FORBIDDEN ACCESS

BLACKTHORN SECURITY
BOOK FOUR

GEMMA FORD

Forbidden Access

Copyright © 2024 by Gemma Ford

All rights reserved.

No part of this book may be reproduced in any form or by any electronic or mechanical means, including information storage and retrieval systems, without written permission from the author, except for the use of brief quotations in a book review.

Mortlake Press

ISBN: 978-1-7385403-5-8

First Edition

Cover design by Deranged Doctor

Disclaimer: This is a work of fiction. Names, characters, places, and incidents are the products of the author's imagination or used in a fictitious manner. Any resemblance to actual persons, living or dead, or actual events is purely coincidental.

CHAPTER 1

This was a terrible idea.

Thorn had known it from the moment she'd been handed this assignment, but her instructions were clear: "Clayton is instrumental to the US government, a High Value Target who must be protected at all costs."

As she parked her car down the road from the Lydian building, she let out an unladylike snort. The guy was a criminal. He'd started his career as a genius hacker, extorting money from people, and gone on to develop an illicit gambling platform and then a new cryptocurrency that fueled illegal activities on the dark web. People had died because of him. Okay, not directly, but the dark web was a cesspool of illicit dealings: weapons, human trafficking, pornography, terrorism.

Why the hell were they protecting this guy?

In reality, she knew why.

He was helping the FBI trace illegal transactions tied to terrorist groups, including those orchestrated by an arms dealer named Aleksandar Markov. Markov had been a person of interest to the U.S. authorities for years, but nobody could pin anything on him. Now, with Clayton's revolutionary new upgrade, they might be able to tie Markov —and a bunch of other bad guys—into any number of crimes.

That meant Clayton had a big red bullseye on his head.

She scowled as she pulled her skirt down and tried to march in these ridiculous heels toward the front entrance of the building. She hoped to hell she wouldn't have to make a quick getaway, because she wouldn't get very far before falling flat on her face.

Better for everyone if Damian Clayton and his shady cryptocurrency vanished, but that wasn't up to her.

Since joining Blackthorn Security as a private operator, she'd traded life as an undercover operative for lucrative private security contracts. Pat Burke, the resourceful ex-SEAL Commander and her new boss, had the inside track to government operations, ensuring his agency handled off-the-books missions for national security. Thorn preferred it to a mundane job on Civvie Street.

"Why the sudden change of heart?" she'd asked, back at the office. Crypto developers weren't known for their altruism or government cooperation.

"He had an attack of conscience," Pat had replied, offering no further explanation.

Thorn scoffed.

An attack of conscience, my ass.

People like Clayton didn't change. They didn't suddenly wake up and think, I don't want to do this anymore. I think I'll turn myself in, cut a deal and go on the straight and narrow. The authorities obviously had something on him, and were willing to overlook it, in exchange for his cooperation.

The Lydian building loomed ahead, a sleek three-story edifice of glass and chrome in Palo Alto. Silicon Valley was now her battleground. It was a far cry from the dusty streets of Baghdad where she had once navigated through market crowds, tailing insurgents without them ever noticing. Here, the enemy wore tailored suits instead of combat gear, and the weapons were lines of code rather than AK-47s.

Thorn walked up to Clayton's building, clutching a manilla folder. Her strawberry blonde hair—a genetic gift from her Scottish grandmother and the one downside to undercover work because it was so noticeable—was pulled back into a stylish chignon.

Her plan—if you could call it that— was to walk right in the front door. She would stride into the secure Lydian building looking like a sexy businesswoman, someone who fit right in at the sleek office block and wouldn't draw any suspicion.

Except, she needed an "in".

Opportunity struck when she saw a frazzled businesswoman in the parking lot juggling binders, coffee, a purse, as well as pulling a suitcase behind her. The woman dropped a binder, cursed under her breath, and stopped walking.

Thorn rushed over, pushing the folder under her arm. "Let me help you with that."

"Oh, thank you," the woman replied, gratefully, as Thorn bent to pick up the binder. "I'm not having a good day." The suitcase tipped over. The woman scoffed. "See what I mean?"

"Don't worry, I totally get it." Thorn handed her the binder, but as she did, she stealthily unclipped the laminated ID card attached to the woman's blazer pocket. Oblivious to the sleight of hand, the woman thanked her before picking up her suitcase.

Thorn smiled and hurried on up the paved walkway toward the entrance. The path curved as it wound through a landscaped garden bursting with colorful flowers and lined with silent oaks gazing judgmentally down. She moved quickly, aware the woman could notice her missing ID at any moment.

A uniformed security guard stood just inside the entrance, behind the turnstile. Thorn assessed him.

Six-foot, two-fifty. Solid build, but a little soft.

Threat level: manageable.

She swiped the stolen ID through the scanner, flashing the guard a confident smile. "Morning, Reggie." His name was on his badge.

"Morning, ma'am," he responded, his eyes on her, not the monitor. The scanner beeped, and she stepped through the turnstile.

A moment later, the guy behind her scanned his card, and the machine beeped again. The guard's focus shifted back to the monitor.

She was in.

Thorn's heels echoed across the bright lobby, with its towering glass ceiling, marble floors, and stark white walls. She barely glanced at the massive bronze phoenix, wings spread wide, rising from the ashes in triumph. Sunlight filtered through the tinted ceiling, making the statue almost seem alive, its burnished surface glowing as if it held some hidden power.

It had to mean something to Clayton—his building, his symbol. Maybe she'd ask him about it, if the opportunity arose.

Thorn scanned the lobby. Only one visible exit—the same way she'd come in. The reception desk to her left buzzed with activity, people getting visitor passes. Above it, a floor directory caught her eye. She quickly located Damian Clayton, CEO.

Well, that was simple.

As expected, his office was on the top floor. She turned and headed for the elevator.

During the ride up, Thorn stayed at the back, silently observing her fellow passengers. Always assessing, always alert. After all these years, she couldn't turn it off if she tried. But this crowd didn't offer much in the way of threats.

The three men were slim, under a hundred and fifty pounds, all wearing eyeglasses—likely from too many hours staring at screens. No muscle, smooth hands, faces etched with the kind of passivity that comes from sitting in a cubicle all day.

She couldn't understand how anyone could find coding appealing—felt like an air-conditioned prison cell to her.

The men got off before she did, leaving her alone as the elevator continued to the fourth floor. When the doors slid open, she stepped into a stylish lobby. No reception desk, no one to greet her—just two plush leather sofas flanking a sleek coffee table. Against one wall, a state-of-the-art coffee machine gleamed on a polished counter.

Classy.

She scanned the room for surveillance cameras but didn't spot any. Not that it mattered—she'd be gone before anyone realized she was a problem. Thorn noted the names on the doors. Clayton's office was right off the lobby, along with the CFO, Michael Ambrose, and the Head of HR, Delia Smithson. Taking a steadying breath, she gripped the handle and pushed open Clayton's door.

Instead of Damian Clayton behind a big wooden desk, she was greeted by a pretty blonde assistant in a sharp pantsuit, her fake breasts strategically highlighted by a white blouse.

Thorn resisted the urge to roll her eyes.

This was just the outer office. Besides the assistant, two hulking security guards flanked the CEO's office door. She sized them up.

Ex-military, three hundred pounds each, definitely armed.

Threat level: high.

The guards gave her a once-over and then relaxed, assuming she wasn't a threat.

BIG mistake.

"Can I help you?" the pretty assistant asked. She had a high-pitched voice like a barbie-doll. Thorn pasted a harassed smile on her face.

"Oh, yes. Thank you. I'm here to see Mr. Clayton." She flashed the stolen ID, praying the woman wouldn't look too closely at the photograph. "Sarah Flannagan from Finance."

Sarah didn't have red hair, but she was auburn, and at a push, the strawberry blonde could be a recent dye-job.

Barbie didn't even glance at it. "You don't have an appointment." The sign of a good personal assistant—she knew her boss's schedule without having to look it up.

"Damian asked me to bring him these figures." She gave a dramatic sigh and held up the folder in her left hand. Her right she kept free in case she had to reach for the Glock holstered to her inner thigh. "You know how he is, wants everything yesterday."

Barbie gave a reluctant nod. "I'll let him know you're here."

"Thank you."

Thorn sat down, observing the guards. They wore earpieces and stared straight ahead, their eyes fixed on some imaginary spot on the far wall. She tapped out a message on her phone to Anna, the logistics manager at Blackthorn Security HQ, based in Washington D.C. Almost immediately, the phone on Barbie's desk began to ring.

She hurried over. "Hello. Mr. Clayton's office."

Thorn waited.

"Oh, God," came the expected reply. There was an urgency to her voice now. "Yes, of course. I'll send them down."

Thorn watched as Barbie hung up, then swung around to address the guards. She kept her voice low, but not low enough so Thorn couldn't overhear. "Someone was seen tampering with Damian's SUV. There's a ticking sound coming from underneath. It could be a bomb."

The guards dashed out.

Fools.

Barbie glanced at Damian's door, as if she was trying to decide whether to inform him or not. Shit. That wasn't part of the plan. She had to distract her.

Thorn rose from the couch. "Something wrong?"

"No. Well, actually yes, but I'm sure it's a false alarm." Her voice was shaky.

"I hope so."

She took a step toward Barbie, prepared to restrain her if necessary, but at that moment, she said, "Excuse me, I'm going to use the restroom."

And leave your boss alone, unguarded.

Perfect.

Barbie might be pretty, but she had shit for brains.

"Take your time."

Thorn waited until she was out of the office, then followed, slipping something from her jacket pocket as she moved. Once Barbie was in the restroom, Thorn slid a small, triangular wedge under the door. She tested the handle—it wouldn't budge. Satisfied that Barbie was locked in, she headed back to Clayton's office.

Reaching under her skirt, Thorn drew her Glock, the cold steel familiar and reassuring in her hand. She paused at the CEO's door, listening.

Silence. He was alone.

Slowly, she turned the handle and stepped inside.

"Good morning, Mr. Clayton." Thorn closed the door behind her and locked it.

Clayton looked up from his desk, eyes landing on the gun. He jumped out of his chair. He was fit, toned, and in great physical shape. Not the desk-bound geek she'd expected.

Six-two, two hundred pounds of lean muscle.

Threat level: moderate.

"Where's Christine?"

Interesting. His first thought was for his assistant, not his two security guards or even himself. Maybe there was something between them. Wouldn't be the first time a CEO got involved with his P.A., and it definitely wouldn't be the last. She didn't care either way.

"Who are you?" His eyes were on the gun. No fear, just anger. That surprised her.

She raised the Glock. "I'm the woman who's going to kill you."

CHAPTER 2

She was expecting surprise, fear, even panic, but she got neither of those things. His expression darkened, and his eyes burned into her.

Surprised, she realized he was angry.

Why wasn't he scared?

He should be. He was about to die—hypothetically speaking.

"Who are you, and what have you done with my men?" he demanded, in a deep growl. Thorn admired his stance—feet apart, leaning slightly forward, hands planted on his desk. It was the stance of a man used to control, a man who wasn't ready to accept his fate. He was a fighter. That was good. He'd need to be.

"Your men are busy investigating a fake car bomb in the parking garage." He winced, realizing how easily she'd outsmarted them. "And your assistant is locked in the restroom. I'm afraid help's not coming."

His eyes flicked to the gun again, then back to her, sizing her up. It wasn't a look of appreciation, he was calculating whether he could take her down without getting shot.

"Don't try it," she warned.

The words hit home, and he sank back into his chair. She didn't believe for a second that he'd given up. He knew this round was lost, but he was already planning his next move. Smart guy.

"What do you want?" he asked, studying her.

Thorn smiled, genuinely this time. The game was over. She'd made her point. She lowered the pistol and gestured to the chair opposite him. "Mind if I sit?"

He nodded, but his eyes stayed locked on her face. Grayish blue, like the sea on a stormy day. The chair she took was lower than his—maybe by design. A confidence booster for him, a subtle way to make those on the other side feel smaller, more intimidated. The Agency used the same tactic in interrogation rooms.

"Sorry for the subterfuge, Mr. Clayton." She placed the gun on her lap. Now came the hard sell. Not her favorite part, but one she'd perfected in the field. Persuasion—an essential skill in undercover work. "My name's Rose Wilde, and I work for Blackthorn Security."

She gave him her real name, though most people called her Thorn. The nickname had started as a joke at the training academy because she could be prickly when rubbed the wrong way, and it had stuck. She didn't make friends easily, but the ones she did were for life.

Recognition mixed with relief flickered in his eyes. Some of the anger dissipated. "You took out my men, distracted my assistant, and broke into my office to prove how vulnerable I am? Is that it?"

He was a quick study.

She spread her arms. "Pretty much. If I wanted you dead, you'd be cold by now."

He clapped slowly, three times.

"Very impressive. So, this is the part where you tell me I should sign the private security contract with your firm?"

"I'd say your life depends on it, wouldn't you?" Pat had pitched it to him last week after an FBI contact introduced them, but Clayton had turned him down, saying he had his own men. Thanks, but no thanks.

At that moment, the door handle rattled, followed by an urgent knock. A male voice called out, "Mr. Clayton? Are you all right?"

Clayton stood up. "Just a moment."

Thorn nodded, watching as he crossed the office with long, confident strides. He unlocked the door. One of the security guards stood there, holding an alarm clock.

"I'm fine, thank you, Stephen. I see you've found the bomb?"

Stephen flushed.

"Could you please let Christine out of the restroom?"

He blinked. "The restroom?"

"Yes, I believe she's locked in."

"Uh, yes sir," came the bewildered response.

Clayton closed the door but didn't lock it. "So, Miss Wilde, what exactly are you offering?"

Thorn took a breath. "A close-protection team of four of our best operatives, all ex-U.S. military, highly trained for this kind of threat. Plus, a private bodyguard who won't leave your side until the conference is over."

He looked skeptical. "I'm a private person. The idea of someone glued to my side 24/7 doesn't appeal to me."

"Neither does being dead, I'd imagine."

He tilted his head. "Touché. And who would be my personal bodyguard? You?" His stormy eyes studied her with an intensity that was unsettling.

She lifted her chin. "Do you have an issue with a woman guarding you?"

He smiled. "I can tell you're very good at what you do, Miss Wilde, but I can't have a bodyguard, male or female, trailing me everywhere. It'll make my shareholders nervous. They're already jittery over these ridiculous death threats."

"Are they ridiculous?" she asked. Pat had warned her Clayton was in real danger, with half the criminal underworld wanting him dead. It was only a matter of time before another attempt was made on his life. "I heard you've already had several close calls."

"If you call someone losing control of their car a close call, then yes."

"You think the near hit-and-run was a coincidence?" According to Pat, Clayton had narrowly avoided being run down by a speeding driver the police never traced.

"Maybe." Then his eyes hardened. "But the sliced brake line on my SUV wasn't."

"I heard you crashed into a tree."

"Shrubbery, actually." He winced. "Softer landing. Luckily I wasn't hurt."

Thorn nodded.

"Do you see my dilemma? The share price is volatile because of the upcoming conference and rumors about my announcement. I can't afford to add to the panic."

"We have a solution for that, sir." She deliberately deferred to him. She wanted to restore his sense of control, to make him feel like the client with the final say. People were much more likely to agree when they felt they were calling the shots.

"I'm listening." He leaned back in his chair, studying her. He looked relaxed, but the tension in his neck and jaw said otherwise.

"But first, I have to ask—do you have a girlfriend?" Pat's background check hadn't turned up anyone significant, but there was always the chance Clayton was keeping a relationship under wraps.

His eyes flicked to the closed door and back to her. "No one serious."

Ha! She'd been right about Christine, but it sounded like whatever was going on wasn't mutual. Unrequited feelings could complicate things. "Good. Then no one will question the appearance of a new woman in your life."

"What?" He placed his hands on the desk. "Wait a minute—"

"Oh, didn't I mention? I'll be posing as your wife."

"Wife?" he blurted out, nearly spluttering. The shock on his face made her smile. Her reaction when Pat first suggested the plan had been exactly the same.

She raised a hand. "I know but hear me out."

He fell silent, though the veins in his neck bulged, and his eyes shifted from stormy to outright furious. He wasn't happy.

"As your wife, I'll have a legitimate reason to be with you at all times. No one will question us being together, and it'll explain away any increased security without raising suspicion."

Clayton's brow furrowed, but he was listening.

"It also simplifies logistics," she continued. "We can secure your home, and I'll be there round the clock without anyone questioning my presence."

"This is a fake marriage, right?"

"Of course." She suppressed a shiver. She wasn't that crazy.

He leaned back, his eyes narrowed. "What about the media? They'll have a field day with this."

"Exactly." A small smile played on her lips. "The media attention will be a distraction. It'll shift focus away from the real reason I'm here—your protection. A high-profile relationship will divert attention from the threats. No one will bat an eye at us being seen together constantly. It's the perfect cover."

He sighed, rubbing his temples. "I suppose it makes sense, but how are we going to convince everyone we're married? I'm a confirmed bachelor." It was said without emotion. He didn't look pleased or displeased by the fact.

"We'll release some staged wedding photos to the press," she replied confidently. "And we'll make sure your inner circle knows first. It's crucial they understand why this is necessary. It'll also give us an excuse to stay home together until the conference, reducing your exposure to potential threats. It's not ideal, but it's the best way to ensure your safety."

He shifted uncomfortably in his chair. "I don't know. I have meetings—"

"Nothing that can't be handled via video call." In today's world, that was a given. "You need to start taking these threats seriously, Mr. Clayton. If I could get to you, so can a trained hitman—and from what I've heard, there are plenty eager to take the job. The price on your head is high."

He cleared his throat. "I see you've thought this through."

She grinned. "Pretty much. Look, I know it's not ideal. Trust me, I wasn't a fan of this plan either, but it's a good one. With your house surrounded and someone on the inside with you at all times, even when you're asleep, no one will be able to get to you. You'll have round-the-clock protection."

He arched an eyebrow. "Just so we're clear, we are not sleeping in the same room. The house is big enough for you to have your own, right next to mine."

"If that's the way you prefer it, sir." She didn't meet his gaze. Hawk, one of the other operatives at Blackthorn Security, had told her how a target had been kidnapped from under his nose in the same hotel just last year. But she got his need for privacy. She didn't relish the idea of sleeping in the same room as this arrogant, bad boy billionaire either.

He sighed. "Okay, fine. I'm consenting, but only because this is so important. My new update will change the face of cryptocurrency forever. It's essential it gets released. Even if something happens to me, the changes must be implemented. If you can guarantee me that, then I'll take you on."

She hesitated. If something happened to him, it would mean she had failed, but she didn't want to think about that. "I'm not sure I can make that promise. No one on our team is qualified to do that." She sure as hell wouldn't know where to begin and she doubted anyone else in the unit would.

"You don't need to know how to implement it," Clayton reassured her. "It's a piece of code that makes changes to the cryptocurrency's default wallet where the privacy features are stored. You must locate the code and give it to James Holloway, the head of my development team. He'll see that it's implemented. I haven't told him where it is for his own protection. It's bad enough having a hit out on me, I don't want to lose my head developer or any members of my team too."

"Excuse me for asking." Thorn tilted her head to the side. "Why don't you just implement this upgrade now and get it out of the way? Wouldn't that mitigate the threat against you?"

He gave a stiff nod. "It would, yeah, but the U.S. Government is pulling the strings here. They've asked me to wait until the global Crypto and Blockchain Summit in Miami. Something to do with setting up a sting operation. I agreed because it is perfect timing. The annual summit is where all new crypto updates are released. Global tech firms from all over the world will be there, reporters will be ready to pounce, shareholders will be poised to act, consumers will be waiting to buy. It's where it all happens."

"Miami?"

"Yeah. It's somewhere different every year. This year it's Florida's turn."

Thorn ground her jaw. Miami added another variable, which meant more potential for things to go wrong. But it wasn't her call. There were forces bigger than her at play here.

"I'll agree to your terms, if you tell me where the code is hidden. I can't pass it on to your head developer if I don't know where it is."

As Clayton had said, only he knew where the update was hidden. Not even those in his inner circle were privy to the code that would peel back the layers of secrecy surrounding the cryptocurrency transactions so that users were less protected. That's what made him such a hot target.

Get rid of Clayton, get rid of the upgrade. Problem solved.

Once the fix had been implemented and the open-source code was available for the world to see, no crypto network would ever be the same again. For many players that meant *Game Over.*

CHAPTER 3

"Smile," Damian muttered, as the limo driver—a former Navy SEAL—approached the gates of his sprawling estate on the outskirts of San Francisco. He scowled at the swarm of reporters who'd gathered outside the property, buzzing with excitement over the news of his surprise nuptials.

"It's not every day one of San Francisco's most eligible bachelors gets married," Thorn said, glancing across at him. He wasn't sure if she was mocking him or not. It was hard to tell with her, there was always this edge of hostility to her voice. Either way, it didn't make him feel any better.

He hated the term "eligible bachelor." Bachelor he could handle, but eligible made him feel like an item of clothing being inspected and tried on by an enthusiastic shopper. Besides, he still wasn't convinced all this was really necessary. It felt like overkill—although, when he thought about the men whose entire criminal enterprises were at risk due to his software update, he suppressed a shiver. Maybe it was.

The fake wedding ceremony, otherwise known as the official briefing, had been held at a downtown hotel, after which a carefully worded press release had been sent out over the wires. He had to hand it to Blackthorn Security, they were a slick organization.

The internet had exploded with rumors, conjecture and wild guesses as to who crypto billionaire Damian Clayton's mystery bride was. The radio stations had picked up the story, whipping up a frenzy of curiosity. Poor Christine was mentioned as a possible candidate, but she would know by now that it wasn't her.

He regretted hurting her, but he'd tried to warn her, to let her down easy. It was for her own good, too. Once he took her out of the picture, anyone targeting him would know she wasn't the way to get to him.

The conversation hadn't gone well.

"I'll be working from home for the next two weeks, until the conference."

"Really?" She'd actually lit up at the prospect. *"Should I come over to your place and work from there?"*

"No. That wouldn't be a good idea."

"Oh? Why not?" The disappointment etched in her face was enough to make him cringe. How would she feel she found out he was getting married—just not to her?

To be fair, they'd only had a casual fling a couple of months back, but he knew she hoped for more, and if he were totally honest with himself, he'd been keeping her hopes up just a little, for those nights when the loneliness set in, and he needed somebody to hold. To hold him. But that wasn't fair on her. He didn't have feelings for her, not like that. Sure, she was attractive, and they had a good time, but there was no spark. She didn't make his blood pump, not like Rebecca had.

His scowl deepened. Why the hell had he thought about her? His ex-wife had been out of the picture for years.

"I—I can't tell you why," he'd said, feeling like a prize prick. *"It'll be announced tomorrow."*

She'd paled.

"There's nothing wrong, is there? You're not sick or anything?"

She cared. That only made it worse.

"It's for security purposes. That's all I can say at this point."

Hopefully, that would be enough. He couldn't tell her any more than that without risking the truth coming out. It had to look real in order for it to work.

His bride's name, along with a carefully curated wedding photo, would be released tomorrow, once they'd had a chance to get them taken. It wasn't Rose's real name, of course. Or her nickname, Thorn, which he thought appropriate. It was a carefully constructed legend, with all the online history and social media accounts one would expect.

Damian had offered the gardens at his mansion for the "official" photographs since they were expansive, naturally beautiful, and backed onto open fields, which in turn were surrounded by bushes and tall trees. The property was easier to secure than a hotel or wedding venue, and the vastness meant it was difficult for the press to spy on them.

His new bride smiled and waved through the bullet-proof glass at the reporters camped outside the gates. He had to admire her poise. Her strawberry blonde hair was piled up in a messy bun with tendrils kissing her cheekbones, softening her features, and exposing the delicate curve of her neck. Her skin was dewy and smooth, and the make-up around her green eyes made them glow like emeralds. She radiated joy. Hell, if he didn't know better, he'd think she was indeed a blushing bride.

Then again, she was a seasoned undercover operator, trained to convince the world she was someone else. She took his arm and smiled lovingly up at him as a photographer stuck a lens against the glass.

Damn, she was good.

He wondered fleetingly how many times had she been in similar position, pretending to be in love with a man in order to fulfill her mission or complete the op? The thought disturbed him, even though it shouldn't.

After the earlier briefing, he'd swapped his work attire for the dress suit he'd brought with him and his personal protection office—it was hard to think of her as that—had changed into a wedding gown. Rented, he'd assumed, or maybe she kept it in the closet for just such occasions. Either way, it fitted her like a glove.

When she'd walked into that hotel suite, he wasn't the only man at a loss for words. She looked fucking incredible, like a model in a bridal magazine. The dress was an elegant, silk creation with a plunging backline and made him want to run his hand over her smooth, bare skin.

The thin straps clinging to her toned shoulders were asking to be slipped off, and he could picture the slinky fabric that clung to her curvy figure falling to the floor. When she walked, the dress swished around her legs, and every now and then he caught a glimpse of a silver strap and coral toenails.

Seeing her in the wedding gown had reminded him of his own wedding. Nine years ago on a private beach in the Caribbean. He'd been younger and full of hope for the future then. His wife-to-be had looked stunning in a similar white silk wedding gown, her glossy dark hair falling down her back. He still recalled the way she'd gazed at him, her eyes brimming with love, not unlike Thorn's in the limo, except with Rebecca, it had been real.

He inhaled sharply as the memory stung. Her friends and family had watched as an unknown computer hacker married into one of America's most nefarious crime families.

But it had all been lies. Every bit of it.

His and Rebecca's relationship. Their marriage. His company's backing by Alek's organization. Nothing had been real. A fact he'd discovered the hard way when it had all come crashing down two days later.

He took a shuddering breath.

Fuck.

Even though this was a carefully planned operation, it brought it all back. Another scam marriage. Another fake bride. He shook his head, the weight of the past dragging him down.

"This must be the shortest engagement in history," he muttered, as they passed through the gates. The wrought iron mechanism closed softly behind them, while two armed operatives faced the crowd outside to prevent anyone following them in.

Christine would probably resign, he thought and immediately felt guilty about his lack of remorse. Shit, why had he led her on? Why had he let her think there was a chance, when there wasn't?

Just in case he got lonely. Horny?

He sighed. What kind of person did that?

The limo dropped them at the top of the driveway, outside the house. Just in case anyone was watching through a telephoto lens, he walked around and opened the car door for his bride.

"Welcome home, honey," he said, earning himself a sharp look. Thorn definitely suited her. Maybe that's why he got a kick out of baiting her. She was always so closed, so controlled that he found himself deliberately provoking her to see if he could get a reaction. So far she'd refused to rise at any of his remarks, which only made him push harder.

She kept her eyes peeled, surveying their surroundings as if she expected someone with a rocket launcher to jump out of the bushes and take aim. To be fair, he couldn't rule that out, but considering the thousands of pounds of security he was paying for, it was unlikely.

Pat had talked him into installing an electric security fence around the perimeter complete with razor wire, remote sensors and infrared cameras. Amazingly, the security company had managed to install it overnight, and were nearly done. Anyone trying to get through or over it would automatically set them off, if they didn't get fried first.

In addition, two armed guards were on patrol at any given time, not that he could see them, but he knew they were there, lurking in the shadows. There were two more at the main gate.

He stretched out his neck trying to ease the tension. All of this, it should make him feel more secure, but it only made him feel trapped.

"It's just for ten days," he murmured as the limo drove away, leaving them alone on the doorstep. Suddenly, he longed for the freedom of the open road. His Harley-Davidson was in the garage, but he only took it out on weekends. It was one of his favorite pastimes and one that he hadn't been able to indulge in lately.

"The perimeter is secure," he heard a tinny voice echo through Thorn's earpiece. It was Hawk, the super-efficient former Navy SEAL who was in charge of the team monitoring the grounds. Anna, their logistics manager, who'd flown in only that morning, was in a surveillance van parked on the property watching the live feeds and monitoring any activity. They had installed several cameras on the grounds, covering the front entrance, the garage, and the patio doors at the back. No one could gain access without being seen.

Damian unlocked the front door.

"Let me go in first." Thorn, Glock in hand, elbowed past him and stepped over the threshold. He let her go, raising his arms. Nothing subtle about this one.

She checked the entrance hall, then the rooms leading off it, including the living room and the kitchen, before returning to where he was standing. "It's clear."

Watching her search the rooms in a wedding dress, holding a gun, was strangely amusing, even though she was efficient, focused and obviously good at her job.

"Something funny?" She turned to him.

"The situation is a little odd, you gotta admit."

She shrugged. "It's work, nothing odd about that."

Definitely prickly.

"Want a drink?" he asked, as they walked into the living room.

"I'm working."

He shrugged. "Well, I need one. It's been a hell of a day." First the sham wedding and then hours in a security briefing.

She ignored him and checked the windows, closing the blinds. He poured himself a glass of wine and sat down on the sofa. "So how does this work?"

She hesitated. "What do you mean?"

"I mean what do we do now?"

"I make sure the property is secure, and that nobody can get to you. You relax and make like I'm not here."

He gave a wry laugh. "Seriously?" A bodyguard was hard enough to ignore, but one in a wedding dress that looked like her... No way. "Why don't you sit down? Take a load off."

"No thanks."

"There are people outside, this place has more security than the state penitentiary. We're safe for now."

She frowned. "It's when you think you're safe that something happens."

He studied her. Stiff shouldered, neck taut, eyes peering through a crack in the blinds. "You sound like you're talking from experience."

No response.

"Thorn?"

"I'm just saying, you can't afford to let your guard down."

Damian took a sip of his wine, his gaze following her around the room. "How long were you with the CIA for?"

She turned sharply. "How'd you know about that?"

"Your boss told me." He shrugged. "You don't think I'm going to have some questions about the person guarding me?"

She gave a stiff nod. "Eight years, but I spent the last five in the Middle East."

Yeah, Pat had said she'd been on some deep undercover mission. "Whereabouts?"

"Afghanistan."

He cocked an eyebrow. "That must have been tough."

She shrugged.

"Why'd you leave?"

A sigh. "Why all the questions?"

"Just making small talk. What else to you talk about with your bodyguard?"

"You don't?"

"Not usually, no."

He grinned. "I've never had a personal protection officer before."

"You're supposed to just go about your business and leave me to it."

Sure, he could go to his study and work, but it felt wrong on their wedding night. How stupid did that sound? They weren't really married, it was just a ruse to deter the men after him. Yet, it still felt rude to turn his back on the woman in her wedding gown standing in his lounge, no matter how much she wanted him to.

Besides, she intrigued him. A woman of secrets, even more than he had and that was saying something. "Why'd you leave the Agency?"

Another hard look. "I got shot."

He sucked in a breath. "Oh, shit. I didn't realize. Were you badly hurt?"

"No. Where's the safe room?"

He'd had it constructed after he'd bought the house, complete with a reinforced steel door. In his line of business, it would be foolish not to. The room was designed to withstand almost any threat.

"Off the kitchen."

"Show me." She was distracting him from the conversation.

As they walked, he scanned her body for a bullet scar, but didn't find one. Her shoulders were perfectly smooth and unmarred, as were her arms, although he could see the muscle definition. She was toned as hell, but that wasn't a surprise. She'd have to be for her work. Her waist was synched in by the dress, accentuating her curves, before flowing to the floor. Tiny diamante or crystal studs caught the light as she moved.

"It's under my left rib," she said, without looking round.

"What is?"

"The bullet wound."

He chuckled softly. "I wasn't—"

"Yes, you were."

Fair enough.

"The safe room is down there." He pointed to utility room on the far side of the kitchen. Thorn marched over and took a look around inside. He heard her descend the stairs to a purpose-built basement and open the heavy, metal door. A few moments later, she was back.

"Good. That's where you go if anything happens," she cautioned, turning back to look at him.

"I'm aware, but let's hope that nothing is going to happen."

"You can't rely on that."

"I don't have to, I have you."

She didn't reply, simply walked past him and back to the living room. As she passed, he got a whiff of her perfume. Intense, but alluring. Like her.

Rose Wilde made a beautiful fake bride. That alabaster skin, wide green eyes, soft shimmering coral cheeks, and of course the soft locks of clipped-up strawberry blonde hair, just enough escaping to soften her prickly expression.

Thorn. Yep, he could see that.

But she was also a Rose, just very well protected.

"Where'd you get the dress," he said, easing himself down onto the couch. "I'm assuming you didn't just have it lying around at home?" He hadn't seen a ring on her finger, but then an operative probably wouldn't wear one, even if she was married.

"Nope." She turned away, not looking at him.

Abrupt. Too abrupt.

"It fits you like it was made for you."

She didn't reply.

"It's yours, isn't it?"

She glared at him.

"Are you married?"

She heaved a sigh. "You ask too many questions, you know that?"

He shrugged. "I'm just trying to get to know you."

"Well, don't. This is not a friendship, it's a job, and I can't do it properly if you keep bugging me."

He laughed. "Okay, I'll stop bugging you, but I'm right, aren't I? You are married."

"Was." She looked him straight in the eye. "He died."

Damian clenched his jaw. "Fuck, sorry."

Again.

He was always apologizing to her. Maybe he should just

keep his trap shut, sit down and drink his wine and try to forget he was once "married" too, but now his life was on the line. Any moment a sniper's bullet could find its mark and he'd die, along with his crypto update. Thorn was right about one thing, a lot of very dangerous men would pay a great deal of money to see that happen. They'd probably put the hit out on the dark web. How ironic would that be?

Except, he'd never been one to sit back and let others do the hard work.

"What can I do to help?"

She looked down at her dress. "Now that is the first sensible thing you've said all day. You can wait here, keep away from the windows, and stay put so I can get out of this dress."

"I had wondered where you were keeping your weapon."

She smirked. He liked the way her eyes lit up. It made a change from the scowling. "The same place I kept it when I broke into your office to kill you."

He snorted.

"Don't move."

He reached for his wine glass. "I won't."

CHAPTER 4

Thorn stood in Damian's bedroom, staring at her reflection in the mirror. She wasn't sure why her chest felt so tight, why there was a sudden heaviness in her throat. A few moments ago, she'd been fine—more than fine. She'd even managed a smile. But now, standing here in this dress, it all felt like too much.

It had been a mistake to wear it.

Do you, Rose, take this man, Jaden, to be your lawfully wedded husband.

Husband.

She thought about Damian and snorted. Not freakin' likely.

Yeah, sure. He was a good-looking man, if you liked that dark, sullen thing—all swirling intensity and black looks. Not her type.

It had been eight years since Jaden had died, and she still wasn't over it. She'd thought she was. She'd convinced herself she was stronger, that she could handle this mission, but the sight of herself in this wedding gown had brought it all back, hitting her harder than she expected.

Pat and the team thought the dress was a rental. She hadn't corrected them. Only Damian had guessed the truth.

But a small part of her had wanted to remember. Wanted to feel like it was her first time again. The excitement, the anticipation, the joy.

Was that so bad?

With a steadying breath, she reached behind and unzipped the gown. It had been the happiest day of her life, after all. She'd wanted a glimmer of that, a chance to revisit it in her memory, a chance to remember *him*.

The silk gown fell to the floor. She'd never find that kind of love again. It was a once in a lifetime thing, and she considered herself lucky to have experienced it once. Some people didn't even get that chance.

Sadly, it had been short lived. She'd lost it a couple of weeks later.

On honeymoon.

The screams still haunted her. She could hear them now, on the beach. The shouts of fear, the cries of terror. Then the gunshots, getting louder and louder. The realization. Running. The hot sand beneath her feet. Jaden shouting at her to get back in the water, gesturing madly. Bullets flying over her head.

Sniffing, she stepped out of the dress. Would the screams ever fade? Did she even want them to?

Thorn shook her head, pushing the memories away.

Sniffing, she stepped away from the gown, leaving it on the floor like a shed skin.

The past was done. She couldn't change it, couldn't bring Jaden back. She had a job to do, and that idiot in the living room was it.

Sure, he was a tall, darkly handsome idiot, with intense gray eyes that seemed to see right through her—but he was still an idiot.

She picked up her holster and Glock, attaching them to her hip with practiced precision. The familiar weight of the gun against her body grounded her, pulling her back to reality. Thorn examined herself in the mirror, now clad in jeans and a black T-shirt, her holster in plain view.

Now she could think like an operative again, and not like a wife.

His wife.

He wouldn't be so bad if he stopped with the questions. She didn't need an inquisition. Steeling her shoulders, she returned to the living room.

She returned to the living room, finding Damian lounging on the sofa, a glass of wine in his hand. He'd removed his jacket and undone his top button, exposing a tanned chest with a smattering of dark hair. He looked up as she entered, his eyes briefly lingering on her before returning to his glass.

"I have to admit, I preferred you in the wedding dress," he said, a hint of a smirk playing on his lips.

She ignored him.

"There's soda in the fridge, if you want something to drink," he added.

"I'm fine, thanks."

She glanced at the nearly empty bottle on the table. "Better to keep a clear head." Not that she cared if he got drunk, but it wouldn't help if there was an emergency.

His expression darkened, but he didn't argue. Instead, he pushed the bottle away, setting the glass down.

"What do you do to unwind, Special Agent Thorn?"

"More questions?" She raised an eyebrow, keeping her tone light despite the tension simmering beneath the surface.

He shrugged, leaning back on the sofa. "What's wrong with getting to know each other?"

Thorn studied him, trying to read the emotions flickering

behind his gray eyes. Was he genuinely curious, or was he probing, looking for a weakness to exploit? She couldn't tell, and that bothered her.

She decided to turn the tables. "How did you get involved in crypto development?"

His gaze sharpened. "You mean how did I become a target?"

She nodded, leaning against the wall, her arms crossed.

"I made the mistake of pissing off some very powerful people," he said. "But you already know that."

"How did you get involved with them?" She ignored the jibe.

He rubbed his temples as if the question pained him. "It's a long story."

"We've got all night."

He gave a reluctant nod. "True."

Thorn sat down on the opposite sofa, her back to the wall. From this position, she could scan the entire room, and react instantly if anyone came in through the door or the windows.

Damian set down his glass. "When I developed Lydian, my aim was to create a cryptocurrency that was truly anonymous, free from the controls of traditional banking systems. I wanted to offer an alternative for people in developing countries, a way to participate in the global economy without the restrictions imposed by their governments."

Thorn narrowed her eyes. "And you didn't think criminals would jump at the chance to use that anonymity for their own purposes?"

He clenched his jaw, his eyes hardening. "Of course, I did. But I thought the good would outweigh the bad."

She scoffed. "That's a pretty naïve assumption for someone as smart as you."

His gaze locked on hers, and she could see the anger

simmering beneath the surface. "Maybe I was naïve," he admitted, his voice low, almost a growl. "But I've learned a lot since then. That's why I'm trying to fix it."

"Fix it?" She tilted her head, studying him. "Or cover your tracks?"

His fists clenched, and for a moment, she thought he might explode. But instead, he took a deep breath, visibly reigning in his temper. "I'm not trying to cover anything up. I'm trying to do the right thing."

"By working with the FBI? Or is this just another deal to save your own skin?"

Damian stood abruptly, his face inches from hers, his gray eyes flashing with anger. "You don't know a damn thing about me, Thorn. You think you have me all figured out, but you don't. I'm doing this because I have to, because it's the only way to set things right."

Thorn held his gaze, refusing to back down. "You don't get to play the victim here, Damian. People have died because of what you created. Innocent people. You don't get to wash your hands of that."

His breathing was ragged, his fists still clenched at his sides. "I'm not washing my hands of anything. I'm trying to make amends. But don't you dare lecture me about morality. I know what I've done, and I know what it's cost me."

She opened her mouth to respond, but the look in his eyes stopped her.

There was more there, more pain, more guilt than she'd expected. He wasn't just angry—he was haunted.

In that moment, she saw a glimpse of the man behind the billionaire, the man who had once believed he could change the world.

He took a shuddering breath and fixed his gaze on her. "You must have done things you didn't want to, for the greater good?"

"I've done things I'm not proud of," she agreed quietly, taking a step back. The air was suddenly charged with a weird kind of tension, and she wanted to dilute it.

Some of the fire left his expression. "Then maybe you should stop judging me for mine."

She didn't reply, and for a moment, they just stood there, unsure where to take this conversation next. Damian took the matter out of her hands. "I'm going to bed."

She got to her feet.

"No, please. Make yourself at home."

"I'd feel better if—"

"I wouldn't. See you in the morning."

She watched him stalk from the room, his shoulders stiff and unbending, his hands clenched into hard fists.

THORN WAITED until nine a.m. before deciding to disturb Damian. She'd heard him rise at five, and from the sound of it, he'd been in his study ever since. After yesterday's tension, she'd hoped for a fresh start, but the nagging feeling that something was off wouldn't leave her. This wasn't just about protecting a high-profile client. There was more at stake, and she needed Damian to take it seriously.

BAD BOY CRYPTO DEVELOPER WEDS screamed the news headlines. She'd just been reading it online, her stomach churning at the words. They hadn't released any photographs yet, those were still coming, but she dreaded having to act like she was the happiest woman alive.

She had been that woman once, but not anymore. Now, the act was nothing more than a strategic move in a dangerous game.

Thorn shut the laptop, her stomach churning. No use dwelling on the past. There were more pressing matters to focus on, like the latest security update.

Blackthorn Security's onsite unit had already been in touch to give her the all-clear. No trouble during the night other than some intrepid reporters climbing the gate, trying to gain access to the property, but they'd all checked out when the team had run their details. No one posing a threat.

The house alarm had remained intact too, affording her a couple of hours sleep. After her big day yesterday, she'd needed it. The nap had soothed her nerves, which were more shredded than she'd realized after tying the knot.

She found Damian in his study, his focus unwavering as he typed away at his laptop. The large, wooden desk that dominated the room was neatly organized, a testament to his meticulous nature. He looked up as she entered, his gray eyes narrowing slightly.

"Do you usually just walk into people's private offices unannounced?" he asked, his lips curling into a half-smile. "Oh, yeah. You do."

Thorn ignored the jibe. "We need to talk about Miami."

He arched an eyebrow, leaning back in his chair. "What about it?"

She crossed the room, keeping her tone professional. "I talked to Pat this morning. The plan is to fly to Miami just before the conference, minimizing the time you're exposed. We'll use an assumed name for the hotel booking, and I'll be with you at all times. It's the safest way."

Damian's gaze flicked to the window, where the sunlight filtered through the blinds. "You really think they'll try something there?"

She nodded, her expression serious. "It's where you're most vulnerable. If I were in their shoes, that's when I'd strike."

He sighed, rubbing the back of his neck. "You've thought this through."

"That's what you're paying us for." She hesitated, then

added, "We'll use your private jet. It's easier to control the environment that way."

Damian gave a curt nod. "Fine. I'll inform my pilot. Anything else?"

She glanced at the map on the wall behind him. It was a geographical map of a region she couldn't immediately place. Beneath it were several framed photographs of people in kaftans and headscarves, their expressions a mix of hardship and resilience.

She'd seen similar expressions before. Afghanistan? Syria? Were *they* why he had the map?

He noticed her gazing at it. "I spent some time there once."

"Where? The Middle East?"

He nodded, but didn't elaborate.

She considered pressing him but decided against it. They were already on shaky ground, and she didn't want to push too hard. Instead, she refocused on the task at hand. "I want to make sure you're ready for this, Damian. The threats against you are real, and they're not going away just because you're in Miami."

He looked at her, his expression unreadable. "You don't think I'm taking this seriously?"

"I think you're trying to downplay the danger," she replied, her voice steady. "But that won't help anyone, least of all you."

His jaw tightened, but he didn't argue. Instead, he stood and walked to the window, staring out at the expansive grounds. "I'm not used to all this—being protected. It feels... awkward."

Thorn crossed her arms, watching him closely. "You'll get used to it."

He glanced back at her, a flicker of something—perhaps

guilt or frustration—crossing his face. "You don't trust me, do you?"

She bit her lip. "I trust my instincts. And right now, they're telling me to be cautious."

Damian turned fully to face her. "I'm not your enemy, Thorn."

She held his gaze, searching for any sign of deception. It was hard to see past his shuttered gaze and creased brow. "Maybe not," she admitted, her voice quieter now. "But that doesn't mean you're not dangerous."

He didn't flinch at her words. Instead, he nodded slowly, as if accepting a truth he'd long been aware of. "Fair enough."

There was a pause, interrupted by his cell phone ringing. Glancing down, he said, "It's Christine."

Thorn nodded. "Keep it brief—and remember to stick to the story as per the briefing."

A droll roll of the eyes. "Don't worry. I know my lines."

She left him to his call, closing the door softly behind her. Instead of going back to the living room, she hovered in the corridor and listened.

"Christine?"

She waited.

"Yes, it's true. She's an old girlfriend I reconnected with recently."

She walked away, already knowing the rest of the script.

CHAPTER 5

Damian went at it hard.

The rhythmic thud of his fists against the heavy bag echoed through the home gym, each punch working out some of his pent-up frustration. Sweat dripped down his face, stinging his eyes, but he didn't stop.

He needed this—needed to feel the burn in his muscles, the sharp ache in his knuckles. It was the only thing that made sense right now.

His life had become a damn circus, and he was the caged animal on display. Everything he'd built, all the freedom he'd fought for, was slipping through his fingers. First, the constant surveillance, and now, he couldn't even step outside without a bodyguard shadowing his every move.

It was suffocating.

And Christine... He hadn't expected her to take the news well, but hearing the hurt in her voice when he'd lied to her this morning had hit harder than he'd thought.

She didn't deserve that.

He'd always been good at compartmentalizing, at keeping

his personal and professional lives separate, but this time, the lines had blurred, and Christine had been caught in the crossfire.

Damian grunted, throwing a series of rapid punches at the bag, each one landing with a satisfying thud. He hated feeling trapped, boxed in by his own choices.

He'd always valued his independence, his ability to do what he wanted when he wanted. But now, with Thorn hovering over him, watching his every move, he felt like he was losing control of his own life.

Fuck.

Thorn was a problem all on her own. She was beautiful, there was no denying that—fierce and capable, with those intense green eyes that seemed to cut right through him. But that only made things worse.

It was infuriating, the way she got under his skin, how her presence in the house made him hyper-aware of every little thing. The way she moved, the way her strawberry blonde hair caught the light, even the way she looked at him —like she was constantly evaluating, judging.

It wasn't just the physical presence that bothered him, it was the constant reminder that he was in danger, that people wanted him dead. It was a reality he'd grown accustomed to over the years, especially working with Alek Markov, but he'd thought that was in the past. Having it thrown in his face every day, especially by someone who was so goddamn attractive, was starting to wear him down. He hated feeling vulnerable, hated the thought that he couldn't protect himself.

He switched to a series of brutal jabs, each one harder than the last. How the hell had he ended up here? The decisions he'd made in his twenties had been bold, rebellious even. Now, they were coming back to haunt him in ways he hadn't anticipated.

He'd been a different person back then, driven by ambition and a desire to disrupt the system. Now, he was paying the price for that ambition, and it was more than he'd bargained for.

Christine quitting had been the final straw. She was collateral damage in a war he hadn't intended to start. He didn't care about most people, but Christine had been loyal, professional. He regretted dragging her into this mess. She hadn't deserved to be lied to, especially not by him.

Damian's punches slowed as exhaustion set in. His muscles burned, his knuckles ached, but his mind was no clearer than when he'd started. The frustration was still there, simmering just beneath the surface.

The problem wasn't just Thorn, or Christine, or even the threats against his life. It was the realization that, despite all his success, he was still vulnerable. That his decisions had led him to this point, where he couldn't trust anyone, couldn't even trust himself to make the right choices anymore.

It didn't help that he couldn't stop thinking about Thorn. Even when she was challenging him, pushing his buttons, there was something about her that drew him in.

Shit. It was maddening.

He didn't need the distraction, didn't need to be thinking about the way her lips curved when she was about to say something sharp or how her body moved with a lethal grace. He sure as hell didn't need to be wondering what it would be like to kiss her, to run his hands over that toned, athletic body of hers.

The punching bag swayed gently in front of him, the chain creaking under its weight. Damian wiped the sweat from his brow, his breathing heavy.

He sank to the floor, letting his back hit the cool tile as he stared up at the ceiling. The storm inside was still raging, but thanks to the physical exertion, it had lost some of its intensity.

Damian raked a hand through his sweat-damp hair. He couldn't keep going like this, cornered by his own emotions.

By the frustrating, undeniable attraction to the one person he should be keeping at arm's length.

Thorn was just doing her job, as much as it irritated him to admit it. If he wanted any chance of regaining control of his life, he'd have to find a way to work with her, not against her.

As he showered, Damian considered his options.

He could ask for another operative, but what would that solve? Thorn wasn't the problem—his situation was. Replacing her wouldn't change the fact that he was trapped in this mess. Besides, as much as she annoyed him, she was good at what she did. He respected that.

No, what he needed was a new approach.

They'd cleared the air, more or less, and now it was time to focus on the bigger picture.

The wedding photoshoot was later this afternoon, and the thought of it made his skin crawl, but it was necessary. They needed the cover, the appearance of normalcy. It was all part of the plan to protect him until he could fix what he'd broken.

He dried off, his mind still churning.

No more dwelling on the past. No more regrets.

No more thinking about his sexy goddamn personal protection agent who seemed to enjoy making his life difficult.

He had to look forward, had to focus on what needed to be done.

CryptoCon was coming up fast, and with it, his moment of truth.

If he survived this, things would change.

He'd make sure of it.

Damian dressed quickly, pulling on a pair of jeans and a simple black T-shirt. There was still work to do before the photoshoot, and he wasn't about to let his frustrations—or his confusing feelings for Thorn—derail him.

CHAPTER 6

*I*t was almost time to get ready. Thorn stared at the wedding dress spread out on the bed and winced. It physically hurt to look at it.

This hadn't been the case yesterday, when she'd initially chosen it for the photoshoot. Back then, it had just been another part of the mission, a piece of the disguise. But she hadn't anticipated the flood of emotions it would unleash. The delicate fabric, the sparkling sequins—it was all too familiar, too personal. Her fingers had trembled as she touched it, the memories swirling back with a force she hadn't expected.

Now, she didn't want to touch it at all. Time had healed that wound—or so she'd thought. But this dress was like peeling off a bandage too soon, exposing a still-raw wound.

Idiot, she scolded herself. She had no alternative, so there was nothing for it. Here goes, she thought, as she picked up the dress and undid the side zipper. Tentatively, she stepped into it, trying not to well up as the fabric caressed her skin.

Jaden, why did you have to leave me?

She pushed the thought away, forcing herself to focus.

She had a job to do. A mission. She couldn't afford to let the past interfere with the present. Not when her focus needed to be sharp.

She heard Damian getting ready next door, his footsteps heavy, his movements agitated. He was probably as eager to get this over with as she was. Each of them wanted this charade to end as quickly as possible.

"He's here. Hawk is walking him over," came the voice in her ear. "Don't forget to take out the earpiece."

"Roger that." Thorn removed the device and left it on the dresser. There was nowhere to keep it in this dress.

She descended the staircase, aware of Damian's eyes on her the moment she stepped into view. His gaze lingered, and she could almost feel the tension radiating off him. He was wearing the same outfit as before—a black shirt, black suit, and a metallic gray tie that matched his eyes. Despite the obvious strain between them, she couldn't help but notice how well the outfit suited him. He cut a striking figure, all sharp lines and restrained power.

The photographer, who introduced himself as Amelio, clapped his hands in joy when he saw them. He'd been told it had rained on their wedding day, so they wanted a few sunny pictures for the family album.

The sun knew its part in the script and cast the back garden in a beautiful, golden glow. They weren't bothering with group photos, since they didn't have a rent-a-crowd. Thorn was grateful for that—taking the deception further with fake guests would have been too much.

"Bellissimo," Amelio crooned as Thorn took her place beside Damian. "Let's go outside. I have found the perfect spot."

Damian took her hand, and they walked stiffly across the lawn. Thorn could feel the tension in his grip, and she wondered if he was as affected by all this as she was.

"You are nervous?" Amelio asked, noticing how rigid they both were. "Don't worry. This will be fun."

Fun. That was one way to describe it. She had to relax, or they were going to blow this. Damian stretched his neck and took a calming breath, his fingers flexing slightly against hers.

Amelio had chosen a beautiful backdrop. At the far end of the property was a serene koi pond, surrounded by vibrant bougainvillea and shaded by a grand, ancient oak tree. Its sprawling branches created a canopy, with dappled sunlight filtering through the leaves.

"Here." Amelio took them both by the hand and positioned them in front of the tree. "It will frame you perfectly."

They stood next to each other. Damian put his arm around her waist. Reluctantly, she did the same, feeling the warmth of his body, the solid muscle beneath his suit. Her face ached from smiling, but she forced herself to keep it up, pretending she was in love. In front of them, the pond's mirror-surface reflected the pale blue Californian sky. She longed to sink into it and put an end to this farce.

"Closer," ordered the photographer, frowning.

Thorn resisted the urge to groan but complied, shuffling closer to Damian until she could feel the heat radiating off him.

"More," Amelio cried, gesturing madly. "I want to feel the love."

Damian muttered something under his breath but adjusted his stance, so she was nestled against him. Thorn inhaled sharply as his scent—clean, fresh, and undeniably masculine—filled her senses. It had been a while since she'd been this close to a man, and the unexpected rush of awareness caught her off guard.

Damian was smiling easily at the photographer, his arm holding her close, almost as if he really were her husband.

With a superhuman effort, she mirrored his expression, though her heart was beating a little too fast, her skin tingling where his hand rested on her waist.

"Perfect!" exclaimed Amelio, clicking away. "Now face each other."

Oh, God. Was this really necessary?

"Damian, take your beautiful bride's hands."

He did so, his grip surprisingly gentle. Thorn noticed the calluses on his palms, the rawness of his knuckles—signs of his recent boxing session. The physical evidence of his frustration made something twist in her chest.

"Look into each other's eyes."

For fuck's sake.

Thorn took a breath and lifted her gaze to his. At first, she saw resistance, but then his expression softened. The steely resolve in his eyes melted into something warmer, more intimate, and she felt her pulse quicken in response.

What was he doing? And why did it feel like her stomach was suddenly filled with butterflies?

"Why are you looking at me like that?" she whispered, trying to keep the tremor out of her voice.

"What?"

"You know what."

A slow smile curved his lips, one that sent a shiver down her spine. "I'm just getting into character. Isn't that what we're supposed to do?"

She inhaled sharply, irritated by how easily he could get under her skin. *This man!* He was infuriating.

But damn it, he was right. That's exactly what she should be doing too.

"Don't forget to smile," Amelio reminded her.

She forced her lips into a smile, feeling the tension in her cheeks.

"That's it!" Amelio gleefully snapped about a dozen more

shots before checking the screen on his camera. "I love it. You guys are such a beautiful couple."

Somehow, she doubted that.

"Now kiss her," Amelio said to Damian. They both turned to stare at him.

"What?" Thorn blurted out.

"We have to take one of the kiss," he insisted, coming over and pushing them together. "It is the most vital photograph of the collection. One you will remember forever. It's the one you will show your children and grandchildren."

She was going to be sick.

"Shut up and kiss me," Damian murmured, his voice low enough that only she could hear.

Her eyes flew to his face. "You can't be serious."

"Let's just do it, then we can go inside."

She sucked in an exasperated breath. "Okay, fine."

"Ready?" Amelio called.

"Yep." Damian lowered his head, his arms closing around her back, drawing her toward him. Thorn braced herself, trying to keep it professional, but the moment his lips touched hers, everything shifted. His mouth was warm, his touch unexpectedly tender. It felt real, and that realization hit her like a punch to the gut.

Her eyes fluttered shut, and she leaned in, waiting for Amelio to say, "cut," or whatever it was photographers said. But the words didn't come, and she found herself lost in the sensation of Damian's lips on hers.

Eventually, Amelio's voice broke through the haze. "Okay."

They broke apart, both taking a step back, as if they'd been caught doing something they shouldn't. Thorn's heart was pounding in her chest, and she had to remind herself to breathe. It wasn't supposed to feel like that. It was just a kiss —a fake kiss.

"Again!"

No.

Horrified, she turned to Amelio to object, but he was shaking his head. "I can't feel the love."

No kidding.

She was about to say they'd had enough, that the shots they had would have to do, when Damian took matters into his own hands. He grabbed her arm and pulled her toward him. Before she had a chance to react, he'd claimed her lips with his own.

This time there was nothing gentle about it. His lips pressed into hers firmly, confidently, as if he was determined to prove something. His hands traveled up her back, his fingers splaying over her skin, sending a rush of heat through her body. Thorn's breath hitched, and for a moment, she forgot where they were, what they were doing. It was just them, locked in a kiss that felt far too real.

"That's it!" yelled Amelio.

Damian released her, stepping back with a controlled calm that belied the intensity of the kiss. Thorn stood there, staring at him, her mind racing. Holy friggin' smoke. What was that?

His eyes met hers, burning with an intensity that made her breath catch. But he didn't say anything. Instead, he turned and marched back to the house, leaving her standing there, trying to make sense of what had just happened.

Thorn was still rooted to the spot when the voice in her earpiece made her start. "Are you done with the photographs yet? We'd really like to get you away from the perimeter and back into the house."

Shit. Had they seen the kiss? Then she let out a slow, measured breath. It didn't matter if they had; it was planned. The photographer had literally ordered them to do it. She touched her ear. "Roger that."

At Amelio's questioning look, she cleared her throat. "I mean, thank you, Amelio. That was perfect."

He grinned and put the cover on his camera lens. "You're welcome. You two make such a perfect couple. I just know you are going to be very happy together."

CHAPTER 7

Thorn had barely recovered from the photoshoot when Anna's urgent voice crackled in her ear, sending a jolt of adrenaline through her. "Thorn, we have an unidentified object flying over the property. We think it's a drone. It could be carrying an explosive device. Better get to the saferoom, stat."

Holy crap.

Drone attacks weren't common in San Francisco, but the world Damian was mixed up in wasn't exactly normal. Who knew what these people were capable of?

She didn't waste a second, barging into Damian's study. His head jerked up, eyes wide with surprise. "We've got to get you to the safe room," she ordered.

He stood immediately, but confusion flashed across his face. "Why?"

"I'll explain once we're there. Now move."

He grabbed his laptop, but she barked, "Leave it!"

"No way." He tucked it under his arm and followed her out of the study. They sprinted down the corridor toward the kitchen, the sound of distant gunfire reaching their ears.

"Is that... gunfire?" Damian asked incredulously.

"Yeah, it's a possible drone attack."

"Shit." His eyes widened.

They didn't stop running until they reached the utility room. Thorn opened the door to the saferoom, ushering him inside before sealing the reinforced door behind them. It hissed as it locked into place, isolating them from the outside world.

"We should be safe here," she said, her breathing heavy as she scanned the small room. It was well-equipped with essential supplies: a first aid kit, satellite phone, and enough provisions to last several days. The air was cool, filtered through a built-in ventilation system, and the console on the wall displayed security feeds from around the property.

Damian leaned against the wall, trying to catch his breath. "What happened?"

"Not sure yet, but we're staying put until we get the all-clear." She moved closer, her instincts still on high alert. "Anything like this happen before?"

He shook his head, the tension in his face evident. "No. I guess they're getting desperate."

"Why do you have such an elaborate setup in your basement?"

He hesitated, his eyes darkening with memories. "To protect my work. I've been developing this upgrade for years, mostly in secret. Only a few of my top developers knew about it. But once it was ready, I let something slip to someone outside my inner circle, and rumors spread. Not long after, I started noticing strange cars following me, hearing noises on my phone."

"That's when the FBI got involved?"

He scoffed. "They actually came to me. They'd picked up chatter from some bigshot mafioso about my work. They offered protection in exchange for my cooperation, but I denied everything. If I'd confirmed it, I'd have snipers after me in the street."

Thorn crossed her arms, studying him. "Which is pretty much what's happening now."

"Only a few key players know about the upgrade," he said, rubbing the back of his neck. "Not everyone."

"How'd the FBI find out?"

"They were monitoring the communications of some bigshot mafioso and intercepted a conversation about it. Didn't take them long to connect the dots and knock on my door."

"Protection is all they offered you?" She raised a brow, skepticism lacing her tone.

"I'm not a criminal," Damian snapped, stepping closer, his irritation flaring. The harsh light of the safe room cast shadows on his sharp features, highlighting the tension between them.

"Maybe not anymore," she replied, her voice dropping as her gaze flitted to his lips, the memory of their kiss from earlier still fresh. She quickly forced her attention back to his eyes. "But you were."

His expression softened slightly, and for a moment, she wondered if he was recalling that kiss too. "How'd you know about all that?"

"I read your file."

His brows shot up in surprise. "My file? I've got a file?"

She looked away, feeling a flush rise in her cheeks—not just from the conversation but from the way he was looking at her. "Of course. Where else are we going to keep the information about you?"

"Can I see it?"

"It's confidential."

He shook his head, clearly irritated. "You won't let me see

a file on myself? I assure you, there's nothing in there I don't already know."

"Then you don't need to see it."

"That's ridiculous."

It was, but it was protocol. Thorn had seen the depths of Damian's past—his ties to Aleksandar Markov, his hacking days, the shady businesses he'd been involved in. But the man standing in front of her now wasn't the same person who'd made those decisions.

"I know what you're thinking," Damian said quietly, breaking the silence. "All that stuff I did when I was young… that's not who I am."

She wanted to look away but couldn't. His eyes held hers, and she saw the vulnerability he was trying so hard to hide. "You're saying you didn't mean to sell people's private data for a quick buck? Or provide a platform for illegal gambling?"

"It wasn't like that." He dropped onto one of the metal benches, resting his head in his hands. For the first time, she saw the weight he was carrying, the regret mixed with anger. "I grew up in the foster system, bouncing from one home to another. The only stable thing in my life was my computer, something I built from scratch with parts I found. At first, I used it to survive, to make a living any way I could."

Thorn's throat tightened. She'd read about his past, knew he'd lost his parents young, but hearing it from him was different. It didn't excuse what he'd done, but it made it harder to hate him. "By hacking into websites?"

He nodded, his gaze still on the floor. "It was easier back then. Security wasn't as tight as it is now." He looked up, the intensity in his eyes making her heart skip a beat. "But I didn't steal money, just so we're clear. I sold contact lists to marketing companies. It's how I bought my first apartment."

She had to admit, part of her was impressed. He'd pulled himself up from nothing, made something of himself. Maybe she'd been too quick to judge.

"What about your relationship with Aleksandar Markov?"

Damian stiffened. "I formed a relationship with Alek's daughter, Rebecca. Not with him. As it turned out, that was a mistake I lived to regret."

Thorn's eyes widened. "His daughter?" This was news to her. Pat hadn't mentioned anything about a daughter. It hadn't been in Clayton's file, either.

"Yeah, I married his daughter. That's how Alek got his claws into me. We were family." A dark look came into his eyes, and Thorn caught a glimpse at how torn up he was.

"I didn't know."

"It's not common knowledge. Anyway, it doesn't matter since our marriage only lasted two days." He gave a humorless snort. "It was shorter than this one's going to be."

He was still messed up about it, she could tell. "It didn't work out between you, then?"

His hands clenched and unclenched. "You could say that."

"How'd you meet?" she asked quietly.

A faraway look came into his eyes. "It was after I developed the gambling site that I met Rebecca. I thought it was a coincidence when we bumped into each other, but now I know her father sent her to seduce me. It had been his plan to recruit me all along."

"Markov used his daughter to get to you?" Thorn's chest tightened at the thought. What kind of man did that?

"Yeah," Damian said, the word heavy with resentment. "We dated for a couple of months, and I fell for her hard. Then she invited me to her father's place. That's when I met Alek and he offered me a job. I was so in love I couldn't see I was being played."

"What kind of job?"

"To help him hide his illegal transactions."

"You mean money laundering." Her tone was sharp, but she couldn't keep the edge out of it.

He nodded, his voice tired. "I was an encryption expert. I knew how to hide things so no one would ever find the trail. That's when I came up with the idea for Lydian."

"Your super-anonymous cryptocurrency."

"That's it. Alek backed me, and a few months later, we had the foundations in place. I released the open-source code and started building it from there."

Thorn listened, captivated despite herself. His story wasn't what she'd expected. It wasn't black and white.

"But after Rebecca… I couldn't do it anymore." The tension in his jaw betrayed his emotions. "I left everything behind."

Thorn wanted to believe it was because he'd had a change of heart, but she wasn't so sure. Yet something in his expression made her think twice. Maybe he wasn't the man she'd pegged him to be.

"I'm surprised Alek let you go," she said cautiously, "considering what you knew."

"He knew I'd be incriminating myself if I talked. Lydian was mine, and nothing could be traced back to him. My silence was my own protection."

"That, I get."

"So where did you go?" she asked, curiosity piqued despite herself.

Damian arched an eyebrow, a hint of a smile playing on his lips. "So not everything is in my file."

She tilted her head, a small smile tugging at her lips. "Not that."

He took a deep breath. "I went to the Middle East."

"The map in your study."

"Yeah. I wanted to get as far away from here as possible. Ironically, I went from one conflict straight into another."

"You went to a war zone?" Her disbelief was evident.

"I fought on the front line against ISIS for almost a year."

Thorn stared at him, shocked. "You? On the front line?"

"It wasn't intentional. I went over there to work on a tech project for the Kurds in northern Syria. I ended up fighting because I had no choice."

Her heart pounded in her chest. This was not the story she'd expected to hear. "What happened?"

Damian leaned back against the wall, staring at the ceiling. "I was met by a man in army fatigues. During the drive into town, he handed me a Kalashnikov and said, 'If you're not dead in two weeks, you'll know everything there is about fighting a war.'"

"But you had no military training."

He shook his head, a wry smile on his lips. "Zero. The closest I'd come to war was playing Call of Duty."

Thorn didn't know what to say. She'd been so focused on his past crimes that she'd missed the bigger picture.

"After eleven months of fighting, things started to settle down. The government pulled me out and put me to work repairing the phone network."

"I had no idea," she murmured, still reeling from the revelation.

"It wasn't in my file because I'd disappeared after Rebecca left. No one knew where I was. I didn't use my passport, didn't take anything that could trace me back here."

Thorn was impressed despite herself. If anyone could disappear, it was him. "And you stayed? Why?"

Damian looked at her, his gaze intense. "Once I saw what they were fighting for, I couldn't leave. The fight for democracy is still going on in Syria, and the good guys are finally winning. I keep in touch with my friends there. They're building something new, something better. How can I regret being part of that?"

Thorn felt a pang of guilt. She'd been so quick to judge him, to label him as the bad guy, when in reality, he was far more complex than she'd given him credit for.

"I'm sorry," she whispered, her voice barely audible.

"For what?"

"For misjudging you. I was wrong, and I'm sorry."

Damian stepped closer, his voice a low rumble. "Maybe we can work together now, instead of against each other."

Her mouth went dry. The way he was looking at her made it hard to think, hard to breathe. She'd been so intent on disliking him, but now... now she wasn't so sure. Not trusting herself to speak, she nodded.

He leaned in, dipping his head as if to kiss her. Every nerve in her body screamed at her to move, to step back, but she couldn't. She just stood there, heart pounding, waiting.

"Come in, Thorn."

The voice in her earpiece jolted her back to reality. She jumped away from Damian as if she'd been burned. What the hell was she thinking? This insane attraction to him was dangerous, irrational. He was her principal, the man she was supposed to protect, not someone she should be fantasizing about.

"Yeah, I'm here," she replied, trying to steady her voice. "Go ahead, Anna."

Damian's gaze remained locked on her, his expression unreadable.

"We've neutralized the threat. You can come out now."

"Okay, great." She nodded at Damian, who moved to open the heavy door. "Thanks, we'll be out in five."

As Damian held the door open for her, he caught her arm,

his grip gentle but firm. "I've never told anyone that before. Please don't repeat it. I don't need the added complication."

"I won't." She hesitated, meeting his gaze. "I'm glad you told me."

His voice was a deep rumble. "So am I."

CHAPTER 8

"It was loaded with explosives?" Damian stared at Hawk. They stood under the cover of the open garage, a space filled with Damian's collection of high-end toys and vehicles. The reality of the threat hadn't fully hit him until now.

"Yeah. We shot it down over your field, and it detonated in the air."

"Holy shit."

"They're getting desperate," Thorn murmured.

Hawk nodded grimly. "We've boosted security around the property and have shooters poised to take down any more drones that might come our way."

Damian ran a hand through his hair, trying to process the situation. "I can't believe this. Alek actually tried to kill me."

"Aleksandar Markov?" Hawk asked, his voice tense. "The arms dealer?"

"Yeah, he's the only one I know who could pull this off."

"Did you get a chance to study the drone?" Thorn asked, her tone all business.

Hawk's jaw tightened. "It was a high-tech model.

Commercial grade, modified to carry a payload. It had six rotors for stability and could fly long distances. The explosive was cleverly concealed to look like part of the drone's structure. It was equipped with GPS, programmed to navigate through the estate's perimeter undetected."

Damian watched Thorn's eyes narrow, her mind clearly racing as she processed the information. "It must have flown in low, avoiding radar and thermal detection. These drones are designed to be quiet, almost silent at high altitudes."

A shiver ran down Damian's spine. The fact that Alek had followed through on his threat shook him to his core. They had been close once, as close as father and son. He had trusted the man—hell, he'd idolized him, seduced by his wealth, power, and his beautiful daughter. Alek had filled a void in his life, a void he hadn't realized was there until it was too late.

"Exactly," Hawk confirmed. "Fortunately, we detected it just in time. Our snipers took it down before it reached the house. The explosion detonated mid-air, causing no damage to the estate."

Thorn pursed her lips, and for a fleeting moment, Damian's mind flashed back to their kiss. There was something about the way she held herself, a mixture of strength and vulnerability that drew him in, despite his better judgment. He still couldn't get her out of his head.

"We need to figure out a way to detect these drones before they get too close," Thorn said, her voice steady. "He might try again, and we can't rely solely on visual confirmation and shooters."

Hawk nodded. "We're working on that."

Damian's eyes shifted from Hawk to Thorn. "Alek won't stop. Once he knows this attack failed, he'll try again."

"There's a lot of money at stake," Thorn agreed, biting her lip in thought. Damian clenched his fists, resisting the urge to pull her lip from between her teeth and taste it himself. "Not to mention that Alek knows that once your update is implemented, he's shooting to the top of the FBI's Most Wanted list."

Damian noticed Hawk's gaze drifting over the equipment in the garage—carbon-fiber bicycles, golf clubs, scuba gear, and more. The toys of a man who was used to living on the edge, who needed constant challenges to keep his mind from spiraling. How long would it be before he got to use any of them again? He ground his jaw at the thought. That wasn't going to happen. He wasn't going to let Alek win.

Hawk turned back to him. "When we fly out to Miami next week, it would be best if we left at 0100 hours. Fewer people around, lower visibility, and reduced risk of an attack. Can you inform your pilot?"

"One in the morning? Sure, I'll let him know."

"Great. You guys get indoors." Hawk nodded to Thorn. "Stay on comms."

Thorn gave a curt nod. "Will do."

As Hawk walked away, Thorn ushered Damian back inside the house and closed the garage door. Just as they stepped into the hallway, Damian's phone began to buzz.

He glanced at the screen. "It's Doug. I need to take this."

"Who's Doug?" Thorn asked.

"A friend," he mouthed, moving into the living room for privacy. "Hey, Doug, how's it going?"

"Hey, buddy. The real question is, what's up with you? I leave for two friggin' weeks and come back to find out you got married? What the hell, man?"

"Yeah, it's pretty wild, right?" Damian sank onto the couch, the weight of the day pressing down on him.

"You could say that." Doug's voice held a note of skepticism. "Who is she? How come I've never met her?"

Damian hated lying to his friend, but he had no choice.

The truth was too dangerous to share. "Thorn's an old girlfriend," he said. "We've been seeing each other for a few weeks now."

"And you didn't think to mention it?"

"With everything going on with Christine, I figured it was better to keep it quiet until we were sure."

Doug paused, processing the information. "It's not like you to date two women at once. I've known you for almost six years, and you've never cheated."

Damian stayed silent, his mind racing for a response.

"How does Christine feel about this?"

He laughed dryly. "She quit. Can't say I blame her."

"And your new wife? I can't believe you got married and didn't invite me to the wedding."

"We didn't invite anyone. We wanted to keep it low-key."

"Well, you sure didn't succeed. It's all over the newspapers. I was shocked when I read it. So, who is she? Can I meet her? When are you going to introduce her to the guys?"

The guys were their weekend rowing crew, the ones who knew Damian better than most.

"We're laying low for now," Damian said. At least that part was true. "Reporters are camped outside my place. I had to get security."

"Serves you right, man."

Damian chuckled, relieved Doug wasn't too mad. Doug was one of the few people Damian could trust, one of the very few who knew about his past. Doug didn't know much about computers—he was a real estate developer—but he had a brother who was in and out of jail and understood better than most the mess Damian was in with Aleksandar Markov. "But I promise I'll have you and the guys over as soon as things settle down. I've got a conference coming up in Florida, then I might take a short honeymoon, but I'll be back."

Alone. He'd have to explain why his marriage had fallen apart in less than two weeks. He rubbed his chin, the stubble rasping under his fingers. Was all this trouble worth it? Maybe he should've just hidden away in Alaska or somewhere and flown in for the presentation. He'd dropped off the grid before; he could do it again. It would've saved a lot of hassle.

"You didn't mention Doug when you gave us a list of names to vet," Thorn said, coming into the living room.

Damian looked up, her presence pulling him out of his thoughts. "I forgot. He was away, and we just hang out sometimes at the boat club."

"The boat club?"

"Yeah, I like to row. It helps me let off steam."

She studied him, her gaze lingering on his chest and shoulders. Her eyes felt like a physical touch, and he had to resist the urge to pull her closer. "You like the outdoors?"

He grinned. "You could tell?"

"You have enough stuff in that garage to start your own adventure company."

He chuckled, appreciating the way her eyes lit up when she smiled. "True. Maybe I'll do that one day. I could use a change of scene."

"I think that's a great idea." Her smile was tentative, but the warmth in her eyes was real. Gone was the prickly bodyguard, replaced by someone he was starting to care about—though he wasn't sure who that someone was just yet.

"When do you find the time to use all of it?" she asked, her body angled toward him as she perched on the couch.

"Oh, you'd be surprised. I don't work all the time, you know."

She paused, her forehead creasing in thought. "I don't understand you. You're a computer geek, but you went to war. You developed your own cryptocurrency, but you also row and ride a motorcycle. How does that work?"

He grinned, leaning back. "What can I say? I'm a complex individual."

She snorted, but he could see the curiosity in her eyes.

"I've always loved the outdoors," he confided, feeling a strange urge to share more with her. "If I hadn't gone into computers... If my life had been different... I'd probably be an engineer traveling the world. There's something immensely satisfying about physically and mentally challenging yourself."

Thorn nodded, understanding in her eyes. Her job required a similar blend of physical and mental resilience, and he could tell she got it.

"Don't get me wrong," he continued. "I love what I do. My brain just works that way—I see solutions where others see problems. But that's only one side of me."

He was opening up more than he ever had with anyone, and it was both unsettling and liberating. Why did it matter so much to him what Thorn thought? She was just his bodyguard, wasn't she?

"What about you?" he asked, shifting the conversation back to her. "You said you were prejudiced because of what happened to you."

Thorn stiffened, her walls going up instantly. "It's not important."

"It is to me."

She turned back to him, her gaze hardening. "Why? Why does it matter? I'm just your bodyguard."

He leaned forward, his voice low and intense. "I see. So you get to question me about my motives, but I can't ask about yours? You bring your preconceived ideas about me into this job, and I'm supposed to just take it?"

She looked away, her jaw tight. "I've been emotional and

unprofessional, I know that. If you want, you can report me to Pat."

"I don't want to report you," he said, his voice softening. Thorn was as closed off as the reinforced door of the safe room. "I want to understand where you're coming from."

She stared at the floor, clearly struggling with whether to open up to him.

"Thorn, I opened up to you," he pressed gently. "Don't you think you owe it to me to do the same?"

Her shoulders slumped, and she glanced up at him, the sadness in her eyes hitting him like a punch to the gut. He braced himself, sensing that whatever she was about to share would change everything between them.

"My husband was killed on our honeymoon. We were at a beach resort in Colombia, enjoying what was supposed to be the happiest time of our lives. The resort was beautiful, with golden sands and turquoise waters, everything you'd expect from paradise. We had only been there a few days when it happened."

"What happened?" he asked, his voice gentle.

"I was in the water, taking a swim, but my husband was on the beach when out of nowhere, a group of armed men stormed the area. They were part of a local cartel, targeting tourists to make a statement. They started shooting indiscriminately. People were screaming and running for cover, but there was nowhere to go."

She shut her eyes, her voice thick with emotion. "I saw him get hit. He died right there on the sand, in my arms."

Tears welled up in her eyes, and she looked away, unable to meet his gaze. Damian's heart twisted at the sight of her pain. He wanted to reach out, to hold her, but he knew that was crossing a line they couldn't afford to cross—not yet, anyway.

"I'm so sorry," Damian whispered, his voice rough with

emotion. He knew what it was like to lose someone, but this… this was something else entirely.

"They said it was part of a wave of violence orchestrated by a local cartel. They were trying to send a message, to show their power and instill fear. It worked. I've never felt so helpless in my life."

"Is that why you joined the CIA?" he asked, understanding dawning on him.

She nodded, her voice barely a whisper. "I had nothing left."

He understood that feeling all too well. After Rebecca's betrayal, he'd run as far away as he could, desperate to escape the emptiness inside him.

"I get it," he murmured. He knew what it was like to be driven by loss, to seek out danger just to feel something—anything.

She sniffed and wiped her eyes, her gaze meeting his once more. There was something different in her eyes now, something raw and real that hadn't been there before. "It was when I started looking into you that I discovered that terrorist organizations, like the ones who stormed that beach that day, use cryptocurrency to purchase weapons. The anonymity enables them to do what they do."

"Except if it wasn't my currency, it would be someone else's."

"I know. Like I said, it was irrational and unprofessional." She took a deep breath, composing herself. "I'm over that now."

Damian nodded, his respect for her deepening. "No one should have to go through what you went through."

"Still, I shouldn't have taken it out on you."

He shrugged, dismissing the apology with a wave of his hand.

Thorn stood up, her movements deliberate and controlled. "So, now you know. Can we move on?"

He cracked a smile, one she didn't return. "Sure. Thank you for telling me."

"Now we know each other's secrets," she said, giving him a hard look before turning and walking out of the room.

Damian watched her go, his mind spinning. He wasn't sure what this new dynamic between them meant, but he felt closer to her now than he had to anyone in years. And damn, if that wasn't a dangerous thing.

CHAPTER 9

Thorn couldn't believe she'd told Damian about Jaden.

She *never* talked about her husband. Speaking his name, dredging up those memories—it was like ripping off a bandage only to find the wound still raw underneath.

The good parts, she kept to herself, like a secret diary hidden away in the corners of her mind. But now, she'd let someone else into that sacred space, and it left her feeling exposed.

Sighing, she climbed into bed, trying to push the day's events out of her mind. But it was useless. From the next room, she could hear Damian moving around—his heavy footsteps, the creak of the shower door, the sound of water rushing down. She imagined him under the spray, water sluicing over his tanned, muscular body, and a sudden, vivid image sprang to mind. His broad chest, the way his muscles shifted beneath his skin, how the droplets would cling to the lines of his abs before sliding down to where the towel hung low on his hips.

What the hell was wrong with her?

She squeezed her eyes shut, willing the image away, but it only grew more vivid. She could practically feel the heat of his body, the strength in his arms. She'd felt it earlier, when he'd held her, his hands firm against her back. It was a memory that had lodged itself in her brain, stubbornly refusing to leave.

She rolled over, trying to find a comfortable position. But sleep was elusive. Her mind kept drifting back to him, to the complexity of the man she'd vowed to protect. He was an enigma—a brilliant crypto developer with a dark past, yet he'd also fought for something good, something real. He'd been hurt, betrayed, and that vulnerability called to something deep inside her.

Damian Clayton was more than just a job. He was a man who had lived through hell, just like she had. And that connection, that shared experience, was dangerous.

She threw back the covers, knowing sleep wouldn't come. But just as her feet touched the carpet, she heard a loud crash from Damian's room. Her heart leapt into her throat.

Grabbing her Glock, she bolted down the corridor and flung open his door. "Are you all right? I heard a crash."

Damian stood there, a towel slung low on his hips, looking sheepish. "Sorry, I didn't mean to wake you. I knocked over the vase, that's all."

For a moment, she couldn't move. It was like her imagination had conjured him right in front of her. His body was exactly as she'd pictured—tanned, muscular, with a smattering of dark hair on his chest. And that towel... barely hanging on.

"A vase?" she echoed, her voice sounding distant even to her own ears.

"Yeah." He gestured to the broken glass scattered across the floor, the remnants of the vase and the flowers lying in a sad heap. "It was dead anyway. I tried to move it, but it slipped. My hands were wet."

She finally managed to drag her gaze from his body to the mess on the floor. Her heart was still pounding, but she forced herself to lower her weapon. "Okay, as long as you're not hurt."

"I'm fine." His voice was soft, and she realized he was looking at her in a way that made her pulse race even faster.

His eyes dropped to her oversized T-shirt and leggings—practical sleepwear for someone always on alert. But the way he was looking at her now made her feel... exposed.

"You got here pretty fast," he said, his tone almost teasing. "I thought you'd be asleep already."

She forced a smirk, though her heart was still thudding in her chest. "It's my job. I should really be in here, protecting you, but I know you don't want that, so—"

"It's not that I don't want it." He took a step closer, his voice dropping to a near whisper. "It's just that I'm a private person. When we started this, I didn't know you very well."

"And now?" She wasn't sure why her voice came out so breathy, so needy.

"Now, I know you much better." His eyes locked onto hers, his voice a seductive murmur.

Oh, God.

If he came any closer, she wasn't sure she could control herself. Her mind was screaming at her to back off, to put some distance between them, but her body... her body wanted to close the gap.

He took another step toward her, and she felt the heat radiating off his skin. "In fact, after everything that's happened today, I think it would make me feel a whole lot better if you stayed."

Her throat went dry, and she struggled to find her voice. "I'm not sure it's strictly necessary."

He grinned, that infuriatingly sexy grin. "You are my wife, after all. It would be strange if we didn't share a room."

"It's not real," she whispered, her voice barely audible. "None of this is real."

He moved closer, his hand sliding around her waist, pulling her against him. The heat of his skin seared through her thin T-shirt, and she couldn't stop the shiver that ran down her spine. "Let's pretend," he murmured, his lips hovering inches from hers. "You're good at that."

Her heart pounded in her chest, her body screaming at her to close the distance, to feel his lips on hers again. She opened her mouth to protest, but the words never came. Instead, his lips crashed down on hers, demanding, hungry.

The world tilted on its axis. His kiss was nothing like the first—this was raw, intense, filled with a passion that stole the breath from her lungs. She gripped his shoulders, her fingers digging into the hard muscle as she kissed him back with equal fervor.

All the tension, the frustration, the anger she'd been holding onto—it all poured out in that kiss. And he matched her intensity, his hands roaming up her back, pulling her closer, closer until there was no space left between them.

Somewhere in the haze, she felt him take her gun and toss it onto the bed, but she didn't care. All that mattered was the feel of his lips on hers, the way his body pressed against hers, hard and unyielding.

She was drowning in him, in the taste of him, the scent of him. He was everything she didn't want, everything she was supposed to resist, and yet... she couldn't stop.

The sharp trill of his phone cut through the fog, and he pulled away with a curse, his breath ragged. "One minute."

He grabbed the phone off the bed, and she stood there, trembling, her mind spinning.

"Hello?" His voice was rough, laced with frustration.

She tried to steady her breathing, to make sense of what had just happened, but her thoughts were a jumbled mess. God, that kiss. It had been... Intense didn't even begin to cover it.

He listened for a moment, his expression shifting from frustration to confusion. "Yeah, she's here. Hang on." He handed her the phone, his eyes dark with something she couldn't quite read. "It's for you."

"What?" She blinked, still trying to process everything. It took her a second to realize what he meant. She'd left her earpiece in the other room, so this was the only way they could reach her.

"Hello?" she managed to croak, her voice still unsteady.

"Everything okay?" came Hawk's voice. "We couldn't reach you."

"Yeah, sorry. I heard a smash and came to investigate, but it's a false alarm. Damian dropped a vase." She hoped she didn't sound as breathless as she felt.

"Okay, just wanted to check in. Looks like the security light has gone on by the pool."

Her heart skipped a beat, and she grabbed her Glock from the bed. "I'll check it out."

"I've asked the guys on patrol to take a look, but they're at the far side of the property."

"Okay, I'm heading there now."

"Stay on comms," Hawk instructed.

Damian watched her, his eyes dark and stormy. "Is there a problem?"

"The security light went on by the pool," she replied, all business now. "I'm going to check it out."

"I'll come with you." He started reaching for his clothes.

"No." Her tone was firm. "You stay here, out of sight. If I don't come back, head for the saferoom."

His jaw clenched, but he nodded, albeit reluctantly.

She took a deep breath, trying to push aside the lingering effects of their kiss. There was no time to dwell on it now. She had a job to do.

Gripping her Glock, she slipped out of the room and into the night.

CHAPTER 10

Thorn moved silently along the darkened hallway, her Glock ready at her side. The only sound was the soft hum of the air conditioning as she approached the sliding glass door leading to the pool area. The automated security light had flicked off again, suggesting that someone might be lurking just out of sight. After the false alarm with the vase, she was back on high alert, her instincts razor-sharp.

She eased the door open, allowing the cool night air to rush in, carrying with it the faint scent of chlorine and freshly cut grass. The gentle breeze stirred the surface of the pool, which shimmered under the soft underwater lights. Everything appeared serene, but her gut told her something was off. The quiet seemed too perfect, too staged, as if the night itself were holding its breath.

Stepping outside, she scanned the area, her eyes adjusting to the dim light. The shadows seemed deeper tonight, the darkness almost palpable. Thorn advanced cautiously, her senses heightened. The hairs on the back of her neck prickled—a sixth sense warning her that she wasn't alone.

As she neared the edge of the pool, a rustling noise to her right made her spin around, weapon raised, her heartbeat quickening.

Before she could react, a dark figure lunged at her from the shadows, catching her off guard. The impact knocked her off balance, sending her sprawling to the ground. Her Glock skidded across the slick tiles, disappearing with a soft splash into the pool.

Shit!

Her attacker was light, agile, and definitely a woman. Thorn's mind raced as she grappled with her, trying to assess the situation. This wasn't a professional hit—the woman's movements were too frenzied, too untrained. But she was strong, driven by a wild, almost feral energy.

They struggled on the ground, rolling over the damp grass. Thorn felt sharp nails rake across her neck, drawing blood, and she gritted her teeth against the pain. Who was this woman? An obsessed fan? Her mind flashed to the worst-case scenarios as she fought to regain control.

"Who are you?" the woman spat, her voice thick with venom. "What are you really doing here?" Her nails slashed out again, this time aiming for Thorn's face.

Thorn ducked, barely avoiding the swipe. What the hell was going on? Her training kicked in as she twisted her body, using her legs to throw the woman off balance. They rolled again, and Thorn managed to land a solid punch to the woman's ribs, eliciting a sharp grunt. But instead of slowing down, the woman seemed to grow more enraged, her attacks becoming even more wild and erratic.

Thorn was losing patience. This was turning into a catfight, and she wasn't about to be dragged down to that level. She needed to end this now, before things got even more out of hand.

With a surge of strength, Thorn threw the woman off her

and scrambled to her feet, muscles coiled and ready. Her opponent was up just as quickly, circling Thorn with a predatory gleam in her eyes. Thorn wiped a trickle of blood from her neck, feeling the sting of the scratches.

"I could ask you the same question," Thorn shot back, her voice steady despite the adrenaline pumping through her veins.

The woman lunged again, but this time Thorn was ready. She sidestepped the attack, allowing the woman to stumble past her before grabbing her by the arm and twisting it behind her back. The woman cried out, but Thorn wasn't in the mood for sympathy.

Seriously, who was this crazy woman? Was she just some unhinged fan, fixated on Damian? Thorn knew Damian had his share of admirers, women who loved the bad-boy-turned-billionaire image. But this was different. This woman wasn't just infatuated—she was dangerous.

The woman swung around wildly, trying to land a hit, but Thorn easily blocked her with a firm push to the shoulder, sending her staggering backward. Thorn didn't waste any time. She followed up with a controlled sweep to the legs, knocking the woman to the ground.

Enough was enough.

Thorn pounced, pinning the woman down with a knee to her chest. The woman struggled beneath her, but Thorn's strength and training easily overpowered her. She straddled the woman, pressing her down into the damp grass. The woman's chest heaved with exertion—or was it fury?—as she glared up at Thorn through the slits in her balaclava.

"Take off the hood," Thorn demanded, her voice icy and unyielding. Her breathing was controlled, steady—unlike her attacker, who was clearly spent.

The woman glared at her, defiance burning in her molten

brown eyes. When she didn't move, Thorn reached down and yanked the hood off herself, ready for anything.

A tumble of wild blonde hair spilled out, framing a furious, familiar face.

Thorn's breath caught in her throat.

"Christine?"

The shock rippled through her like a tidal wave, almost knocking the breath from her lungs. Damian's personal assistant, the woman who had quit just days ago, was the last person Thorn expected to see under that hood.

Christine's face twisted with rage and something else—betrayal. "You think you can just waltz into his life and take what's mine?" she hissed, her voice laced with bitterness.

Thorn's mind raced, trying to piece together what the hell was going on. "What are you talking about?" she demanded, though a part of her already knew. Christine wasn't just angry—she was jealous, unhinged.

"Damian was mine!" Christine spat, her eyes wild. "He was supposed to marry me, not some... bodyguard."

Thorn's heart pounded in her chest as the pieces clicked into place. Christine's jealousy had driven her to this, to attack the very person she saw as her replacement. Thorn stared down at her, seeing the fury in Christine's eyes and her gut twisted.

But she wasn't going to get sentimental.

With a swift, decisive move, she tightened her grip, holding Christine immobile. "You're making a mistake, Christine," she said, her voice even, but not unsympathetic. "This isn't the way."

But Christine was too far gone to listen. Before Thorn could react, Christine bucked wildly beneath her, her fingers clawing at Thorn's arms, scratching deep. Thorn hissed in pain but held firm, refusing to let go. She needed to keep control, to stop this from spiraling further out of control.

With a final, powerful shove, Thorn forced Christine's hands down, pinning them to the ground. "Enough!" she growled, her voice carrying an authority that left no room for argument.

Christine froze, her chest heaving as she glared up at Thorn, her eyes filled with rage and something else—desperation. "I saw you," Christine whispered, her voice trembling with the effort to hold back tears.

Thorn frowned. "What are you talking about?"

"The kiss," Christine said, her voice breaking. "Through the window. I saw it all." The bitterness in her voice cut through the night air, sharp and raw.

Thorn's heart skipped a beat. She hadn't realized anyone was watching. "Christine, I—"

But Christine wasn't listening. The fight drained out of her, replaced by a deep, soul-crushing sorrow. She stopped struggling, her body going limp beneath Thorn's weight. "It wasn't supposed to be like this," she sobbed, the anger in her eyes replaced by tears. "I wasn't supposed to lose him."

Thorn hesitated, then slowly eased off her, still wary but softened by the raw pain she saw in Christine's face. For all her fury and misguided actions, this woman was hurting deeply, mourning the loss of something she could never get back.

Christine's sobs came harder, her shoulders shaking as she crumpled to the ground, the weight of her grief too much to bear. "I loved him," she whispered, her voice ragged. "I still love him."

Thorn knelt beside her, placing a hand on her back, trying to offer some small comfort. She wasn't used to this, to comforting an enemy, but in that moment, Christine didn't feel like one. "I know," Thorn murmured, the lie catching in her throat. "I know you do."

Christine looked up at Thorn, her tear-filled eyes

searching for something, some glimmer of hope, some chance that it wasn't true. "You married him," she choked out, the words filled with disbelief and anguish. "How could you?"

Thorn's heart ached, but she forced herself to stay composed. This was the hardest part of the job—lying, pretending to be someone she wasn't, even when it tore at her insides. "It happened quickly," she said, keeping her voice soft. "We… we reconnected, and things just… fell into place."

Christine's sobs intensified, the reality of the situation crashing down on her. "I can't believe it," she whispered, shaking her head. "I never thought he'd move on so fast… not after everything."

Thorn swallowed the lump in her throat, her heart twisting with guilt. She couldn't tell Christine the truth, not now, not ever. "I'm sorry," she said, the words hollow, but all she could offer.

For a long moment, they stayed there, Christine weeping quietly into her hands, Thorn kneeling beside her, not saying anything more. There was nothing to say that would make this right.

Finally, Christine's sobs began to subside, her body exhausted from the emotional storm. She wiped her tear-streaked face, her eyes red and puffy. "I didn't mean to…" She trailed off, her voice weak and spent.

"It's okay," Thorn said softly, helping her to her feet. "Let's get you inside."

Christine didn't resist as Thorn led her toward the house, her steps slow and heavy, the fight completely gone from her. Thorn stayed close, keeping a firm but gentle hold on her arm, guiding her through the door.

CHAPTER 11

*D*amian couldn't believe his eyes when he saw Thorn dragging his bedraggled assistant into the house through the patio doors.

"Christine? What are you doing here?"

"She was the one who set off the security light." Thorn threw the hood on the floor. "And knocked my gun into the swimming pool."

"You can let go now," Christine sniffed, wriggling her arm free.

Damian nodded at Thorn, who had a bright red scratch on her neck, compliments of his ex, no doubt. Christine, on the other hand, didn't have a scratch on her, despite being out of breath. Thorn must have easily subdued her, without having to land a blow.

Thorn released Christine's arm.

Damian couldn't decide who looked the wildest. Christine, with her usually sleek blonde hair an utter mess, shooting daggers at him, or Thorn with her strawberry blonde locks cascading down her back and over her shoulders like a glorious fiery waterfall, her emerald gaze simmering with annoyance.

"Damian, what are you doing here?" Thorn turned to face him, her hands on her hips. "I told you to stay in your room."

Christine's eyes widened.

"Thought you might need some help." Ignoring her advice, he'd gotten his gun and followed her out onto the patio. He heard the scuffling by the pool and figured Thorn might be in trouble, but by the time he'd gotten to the patio, she'd been striding inside, pulling Christine with her.

"I'm fine."

"I can see that."

"Damian, what the hell is going on?" Christine demanded. "Who is this woman and why is she ordering you around?" Her gaze dropped to his weapon. "And since when do you carry a gun?"

He sighed and glanced at Thorn for guidance.

Now what?

"Why are you looking at her?" Christine snapped, her voice rising. "I'm the one asking the question."

Thorn threw up her hands. "You may as well tell her, although it's going to complicate matters. I'll let the others know we've been compromised, and then I'm going to retrieve my Glock." Spinning on her heel, she marched outside again. Damian thought he heard her mutter something along the lines of 'stupid bitch,' but he couldn't be sure.

"Damian?" Christine's voice quivered, her eyes narrowing. "What's going on?"

"It's a cover, Christine. You are right, she's not my wife. It was all a scam, a ruse for the newspapers."

"I knew it!" Triumph gleamed in her eyes before they clouded over with confusion and hurt. "But I saw you two kissing. If it isn't real—" She petered off.

He sighed, relieved Thorn wasn't in the room. "It's complicated."

Her lip quivered. "Do you love her?"

Love?

The thought made his chest tighten.

"No, don't be ridiculous. She's my bodyguard."

Christine shook her head. He didn't blame her for being confused. He was confused as hell too.

"Why didn't you tell me? Why'd you lock me out? Didn't I deserve to know?"

"Not about this," he said quietly.

She frowned, tears welling up. "I don't understand. What's going on, Damian? Are you in some kind of trouble?"

"You could say that." He shook his head. By coming here, she'd put herself in danger. "Let's sit down, and I'll try to explain."

He wouldn't tell her everything, that would be foolish, just enough so that she would back off and leave him alone until after the conference.

"I'm going to make an announcement at CryptoCon. Lydian will become more transparent, potentially exposing the identities of everyone using the cryptocurrency, particularly on the dark web."

She stared at him as the gravity of his words sunk in.

"It's made me a target. There have been threats."

She gasped. "I thought the bomb threat was a false alarm. Some sick joke."

"It was, but there was the crash a couple of weeks back when I drove off the road, remember?"

"You said your brakes failed."

"My brake lines were cut," he corrected. "My vehicle was sabotaged, Christine."

Her mouth fell open.

"Only this morning, there was a drone attack on my house."

She glanced up, horrified. "What? Here?"

He nodded. "It was loaded with explosives. My security team shot it down before it could do any damage."

She gulped nervously. "I had no idea."

"I know, and that's my fault. I couldn't tell you because I didn't want to put you in danger. The fake wedding was an attempt to protect you."

"Protect me?" Her eyes glistened. "Then—Then you do care?"

He shook his head, trying to be gentle but firm. He wasn't going to lead her on, not anymore. "I care about what happens to you, but you know as well as I do, it was just a fling."

"It wasn't for me," she whispered, her voice breaking.

He felt a pang of guilt but knew he had to come clean. "I shouldn't have led you on. I've put you in danger, and for that, I'm truly sorry."

She sucked in a breath. "What do you mean, you've put me in danger?"

Christ, she was naïve. "Don't you get it? The people who are trying to kill me are ruthless. If they think we're involved, they might try and use you to get to me. That's why the office has been shut down, and the developers are in lockdown. That's why there are FBI agents guarding the building, and why I have a private security company at my premises."

"And why you have a female bodyguard in your house?" Her gaze narrowed, but then she hesitated. "She's the woman that came to your office. She locked me in the restroom."

"I know." He sighed. "She was making a point. She was showing me how easy it was to get to me."

Christine let out a sob. "That was my fault. I didn't suspect a thing."

"It was not your fault," he reassured her as tears welled in her eyes. "You are not trained to look out for assassins. This has nothing to do with you."

Her lips quivered. Please don't cry, he thought.

Too late. Tears overflowed and rolled down her cheeks. She looked so forlorn, he reached out and gave her arm a squeeze. With a sob, she turned and buried her face in his chest.

Dammit. He could handle most things, but a woman crying really got to him. He wrapped his arms around her and gave her a hug. That's when Thorn walked in, followed by Hawk.

CHAPTER 12

No, don't be ridiculous. She's my bodyguard.

The words stung, even though she knew they were true. That's all she was to him—a protector. So why did hearing them leave such a sour taste in her mouth?

She had no claim to him, even if their kiss had been… What? Explosive? Enlightening? Earth-shattering?

Goddamn it. She shook her head, wishing she hadn't heard that.

And now Damian's arms were wrapped around Christine, in the same way he'd held her not so long ago.

It just kept getting worse.

Hawk, who'd stepped in with her, assessed the situation. "We can't let her go now. She's a liability."

"What?" Christine looked up, panic in her eyes.

"I've called the FBI. They're going to take you to a safehouse."

"A safehouse?" Christine's voice trembled. "But I want to go home."

"You should have thought about that before you broke

into a guarded property and jumped a personal protection officer," Thorn retorted, her tone crisp—because of him.

Christine blinked, looking every bit the damsel in distress. "But I didn't know. I thought... I don't know what I thought, but I had to come here and see for myself if it was true."

Thorn did feel a twinge of sympathy. Christine had been Damian's plaything, then discarded—but not entirely—and now she'd found out he'd married someone else.

To be fair, that would irk anyone. She'd want to know what the hell was going on too.

But to find out it was a ruse? The poor girl's head must be spinning. It was enough to confuse anyone.

"You'll be taken to a secure safehouse where you'll be guarded until this is over," Hawk continued, turning to Damian. "We might also need to discuss moving you to a different location."

Damian scowled. "Why? I thought you said it was safer to stay here."

Thorn glanced at Christine. "Hawk's right. If she can get to you, others can too. This place is too big for one team to protect, even with the electric fence and additional patrols. Now that we know they're using IEDs carried by drones..." She shrugged, letting the implication hang in the air.

"We underestimated their skill," Hawk said. "But let's get her someplace safe, and then we'll talk about you."

Christine's lip quivered on cue, and she clutched at Damian.

Give me a freakin' break.

Damian held her at arm's length. "It's only until the conference."

"What about my things?" Christine asked, her voice trembling.

"We'll send someone to your apartment to get them," Hawk added.

Damian let her go. "I'm sorry, but it's for the best, Christine."

Thorn watched her face crumple. They couldn't risk Christine talking to the media—or anyone else—about his fake marriage. Not only would it put her in the firing line, but it would compromise Damian too. He had to be kept safe at all costs. The FBI was counting on them to deliver him in Miami, next Tuesday. A week to go, then this would all be over.

"Let's get her out of here," Thorn said, when Christine looked like she might dissolve into tears again. "We can't afford any more distractions."

Even now, Hawk was away from his post, and the two men patrolling the perimeter had split up, one covering the front gate, the other watching the security cameras positioned around the property.

Hawk took a frightened Christine by the arm.

"I'm sorry," she whimpered, turning her doe-eyes toward Damian.

He gave a tight nod. "I know. Take care, Christine."

Thorn watched as Damian's assistant was led from the house. Once she was gone, Thorn closed and locked the patio doors, before resetting the alarm.

"Are you okay?" Damian asked, his gaze dropping to her neck.

"Yeah, why wouldn't I be?"

"She scratched you pretty bad."

Shit, she'd forgotten about that. "I'll go and see to it," she said, turning to walk out of the room.

"This is my fault." Damian's low growl caused her to pause. "If I hadn't led her on—"

Thorn didn't turn around. "Yeah, well, it's done now.

Nothing we can do about it. At least we got her before she jeopardized the entire operation."

He didn't respond, so she kept going toward the guest bathroom.

WHAT A MESS.

Thorn inspected the nail marks on her neck and flinched. The stupid woman had drawn blood. Hopefully, it wouldn't scar. She cleaned the wounds thoroughly, then applied some disinfectant spray she'd brought with her, just in case.

Damian was right. This was his fault—but it was also theirs.

Christine had been impulsive and acted irrationally, but Thorn totally understood why. The poor woman had been left in the dark, not knowing how Damian felt about her. Then, when he'd suddenly gotten married, she'd fallen apart. Under the circumstances, Thorn could sympathize with her desire to find out the truth.

When she'd asked Damian if he had a significant other, he'd said nobody serious. Well, he'd forgotten to mention that "nobody" didn't view their relationship quite the same way he did.

For Christine, it had been serious.

She'd developed feelings for Damian, and even though Thorn had suspected as much, she hadn't realized how deep those feelings ran.

Bat-shit crazy deep.

Thorn glanced at her reflection in the mirror, feeling a pang of guilt. Her lips could still taste him; her skin felt scorched where he'd touched her.

Another line she'd crossed.

That kiss—oh my God, that kiss—had been a mistake. A ginormous lapse in judgment.

Why? What was it about him that made her react so irrationally? She thought about Christine. Maybe that was just the effect he had on women. He was the spikey, dangerous rock that they smashed themselves against, driven to a frenzy by his stormy gaze and lethal charm.

She gritted her teeth. That meant she was no different than his assistant. No more immune than Christine was.

Thorn inhaled deeply, then blew out the air, forcing herself to relax.

One week, then they'd fly to Miami, and she could put this behind them. She removed a blade of grass from her hair. All she had to do was keep Damian alive long enough to install his crypto update. A task that was getting increasingly more difficult with each passing day.

Damian was waiting for her when she came out. "Thorn, can we talk?"

"About what?"

He hesitated. "About what happened earlier, in the bedroom."

"Oh, you mean that kiss? I thought that meant nothing."

His eyes narrowed. "You overheard?"

She shrugged. "Forget it. It's not important."

His voice was a low rumble. "You know I had to say that. It didn't feel like nothing to me."

She sighed, feeling the sense of responsibility press down on her. "Look, it was a moment of weakness on my part. I should never have allowed that to happen. It's against all the rules."

"Bullshit. I—"

"Forget about it, Damian," she said softly, cutting him off. "It should never have happened. I could get fired if the others find out. Thank God you managed to shut her up in time."

"They won't find out," he said quietly. "Not from me, anyway."

Christine might still mention it, but an FBI agent was unlikely to care. "My only focus now is to get you somewhere safe so I can keep you alive until you get to Miami."

He glared at her for a long moment. "Why are you being like this?"

"Like what? This is who I am. My job is to protect you, and that's what I'm going to do."

He hissed out a breath. "Was it Christine? Are you worried I've still got feelings for her?"

She scoffed, masking the ache in her chest. "No, of course not. I know she meant nothing to you."

He frowned. "I wouldn't go so far as to say she meant nothing."

"Well, I know it obviously wasn't as serious for you as it was for her."

He stood very still, his eyes darkening to a gunmetal gray. "If you know it wasn't serious, why are you pulling away from me?"

She took a deep breath, trying to steady herself.

Pulling away from me.

Why did he have to make it sound so... intimate?

"Like I said, Damian, it should never have happened. There's nothing to pull away from. I'm sorry about that, but can we please just move on?"

His eyes probed her face, then finding nothing, he gave a tight nod. "If that's the way you want it, sure. No problem."

"Good."

"Fine."

She stood in the corridor and watched him march past her to his bedroom. A moment later, the door shut, and she heard him lock it from the inside. The sound of the key turning felt as final as a pin being pulled from a grenade.

An icy chill clutched at her heart.

Why'd she feel so… bereft?

She let out a long, slow breath, then turned to check the alarm system.

Focus. She had work to do.

No more distractions.

CHAPTER 13

The sound of the helicopter's rotors grew louder as it descended toward the helipad, whipping the surrounding trees into a frenzy. The powerful downdraft flattened the grass, sending leaves and debris swirling through the air.

Thorn shielded her eyes from the blinding dust as the helicopter touched down, its skids settling firmly on the ground. They'd opted to take off from a nearby hospital, not wanting to make it obvious to anyone watching the house that they were leaving.

Hawk had driven them to the hospital in the Blackthorn Security van, while two FBI operatives—vaguely resembling Thorn and Damian in height and build—had moved into Damian's house to make it appear like they were still there. It wouldn't fool anyone for long, but a few days was all they needed.

She turned to Damian, who stood beside her with his travel backpack slung over one shoulder. His eyes were focused and determined, but she could see the tension in his jaw. They had packed light—only what they could carry and what was absolutely necessary for the days ahead.

They were posing as backpackers, traveling through Mexico before heading south to Central America and beyond. Innocent, guileless, with no set agenda.

If only...

Her pack was strapped tightly to her back, filled with essentials and gear she might need in a pinch and Anna had given her an untraceable burner to use when she got there. Only for emergencies.

"Ready?" Thorn shouted over the deafening roar of the rotors.

Damian nodded, gripping the strap of his backpack. Without another word, they sprinted toward the helicopter, their footsteps pounding against the concrete helipad. The pilot, a stern-faced man in dark aviators, gave them a quick nod as they approached.

Thorn reached the helicopter first, tossing her backpack inside before turning to help Damian. He handed her his pack and climbed in after her, the wind tugging at their clothes as they ducked under the spinning blades.

Once inside, Thorn slammed the door shut and secured their bags, checking to make sure everything was in place, just as she'd done multiple times before on her way to Kabul from the Afghan airbase.

The pilot didn't waste any time. As soon as they were strapped in, the helicopter lifted off, leaving the city behind. Thorn glanced out the window, watching the ground fall away beneath them. They were heading to a small Mexican village where they could lie low until the summit.

She turned to Damian, who was staring out the opposite window, lost in thought. How did he feel about leaving his home, not knowing if he'd ever make it back there? Apart from the pensive look, he seemed fine. Composed, collected, calm. Even with the threats and sudden departure, he was keeping it together.

The guy was tough; she'd give him that much.

As the helicopter soared through the night, she thought about what lay ahead. The conference was only a week away.

Somehow, she would keep him safe until then. She had to, or the bad guys would win, and Damian would be dead. A pang of something she couldn't decipher hit her full in the chest, and she took a shuddering breath.

Failure was not an option.

The sun had yet to poke its head above the surrounding mountains when the helicopter touched down on a dusty field on the outskirts of a quaint Mexican village called Las Piedras.

"Let's go," Thorn called, and they ducked under the spinning blades and sprinted away from the chopper.

Anna had found the most remote, unassuming village she could. It was off the beaten track, so it was unlikely to be frequented by mainstream tourists or have any internet cafes, WiFi, or CCTV. No way for anyone to spy on them.

They could see the ghostly shadow of a town from the clearing where the chopper had dropped them. It was nestled in a valley surrounded by rugged mountains, hence its inaccessibility. "The only way in is by car over the mountain pass," Anna had told them prior to leaving. "You should be safe there for a while."

Damian set off in the direction of the town, taking big, determined strides. Thorn had a map folded up in her jacket pocket since reception in the mountains would be nonexistent, but she didn't need to use it.

"Okay," Thorn muttered to herself as she set off after him along the well-worn track. They hadn't spoken much on the flight over, which suited her fine. After their last brief discussion, he'd withdrawn into himself, and she'd gone about the business of guarding him without distraction. It was better this way.

It didn't stop the unwanted thoughts, however, and every now and then when he glanced at her, she saw the hurt and anger in his gaze. Slanting silver daggers that pierced her heart—but not enough to make her relent.

He'd get over it, just like he got over his other women. One kiss. Okay, two if you count the wedding shot. Two kisses did not make for a relationship, and they sure as hell didn't mean it was love—or even like, for that matter.

Just lust, the annoying voice in her head said.

Still, the stony silence was better than heated gazes and overwhelming desire that left her breathless and unable to concentrate on her job.

Eventually, they reached a series of dusty outer streets that narrowed as they reached the town. Damian stopped, turning into the rising sun. It cast his face in a warm, orange glow and made his eyes shine with a metallic glint. Her stomach tightened.

He wasn't out of breath, even though they'd been walking for over an hour. He really was an outdoorsy guy.

"What's the name of the hotel?" he asked her, putting his hands on his hips.

She consulted the details Anna had sent her on her phone. "Hostal Las Sabinas. It should be next to the town square."

He gave a stiff nod and set off again, marching down the dusty street that led into the maze of brightly colored adobe buildings, some of which were still in shadow, some of which shone vibrantly in the morning glow.

"We're supposed to be casual travelers," Thorn pointed out, catching up with him. "Slow down. What's the hurry?"

She saw his shoulders tense, but he slowed his pace. Together, they ambled toward the town square—weary backpackers, fresh off the bus from Mexico City. Unsurprisingly, it was still deserted. Thorn looked around, doing a mental risk assessment. The only sound came from a weathered stone fountain, where a trickle of water fell from the figure's urn and pooled around her.

"That's it," she murmured, spotting a small, unassuming hotel situated at the edge of the square. It might have been pretty once, but the whitewashed walls were dirty, and the flowers in the hanging baskets outside had long since wilted and died.

They went around the back into a cobbled alleyway and knocked on the large wooden door. It was early, but presumably, someone would be there since it was a hotel.

Sure enough, a short while later, they heard footsteps inside, and a middle-aged woman opened the door. "¿Sí?"

They didn't have prebooked accommodation, preferring not to leave a paper trail. Not even in a false name. It was best if they were spontaneous, just like backpackers would be. That way, nobody would know their itinerary.

Thorn cleared her throat and said, "Do you have a room?"

The woman stared at her. "¿Qué?"

She glanced at Damian. They were supposed to be American backpackers, but this region was very remote.

She was about to try again in halting Spanish when Damian stepped forward and said, "Buenos días, ¿quisiéramos reservar una habitación?"

Thorn stared at him. Okay, so he could speak Spanish like a native. Seems there were a lot of gaps in his file.

The woman broke into a broad grin and nodded.

Thorn sighed in relief.

"¿Para cuántas personas?"

Damian replied, "Para dos, con dos camas y baño completo."

Thorn thought she picked up *bedroom* and *bathroom*.

Damian said something else she couldn't understand, but the woman was nodding.

"Sí." She held open the door.

They were in.

"I asked for breakfast to be included," Damian said, as they followed the woman to their room. "I thought if we didn't have to go out to eat in the morning, it would make us less conspicuous."

"Good thinking."

People noticed strangers, and in this town, they would be very noticeable. In retrospect, somewhere busier might have helped them blend in more.

Still, the chances of anyone finding them here were very remote, and the backpacker legend was a good one. It gave them an excuse to wander around aimlessly, eating on the cheap and lying low. A couple of days was all they needed before they'd head to Miami for the conference.

"Where'd you learn to speak Spanish?" she asked, once they'd gotten to their room. It was clean and comfortable, if a little sparse, and contained only the bare minimum of furniture. There was no television, no WiFi, and barely any cell phone reception.

Perfect.

"One of my foster families was fluent," he replied, vaguely.

"Why didn't you say?"

He gave the first hint of a smile since they'd arrived. "Didn't want to spoil the surprise."

She snorted. At least he hadn't lost his sense of humor. She took that to be a good sign.

"I'll take this side." Thorn placed her pack on the bed. It was a small double that dipped in the middle, but the bedding looked clean. She wanted to be closest to the door in case anything came through it in the night.

"Works for me," Damian said, walking over to the window, about to push open the shutters.

"Don't!" Thorn shot away from the bed. "You shouldn't do that. You never know who's waiting outside with a sniper rifle."

He sighed and stepped back, but she noticed the flicker of concern in his eyes. He knew she was right. Even out here, in the middle of nowhere, someone could be watching.

"I didn't think."

"You don't have to think about it. That's why I'm here. Stand back." He moved out of the window's line of sight so she could open the shutters. Sunlight streamed in, lighting up the sparse room and pooling on the threadbare rug.

"Nice view," he muttered, gazing out at the town square.

The plaza was charmingly rustic, typical of a small Mexican village. The surrounding buildings had weathered, whitewashed walls, clay-tile roofs, and wooden shutters. Some were modest eateries with a few tables outside under faded umbrellas. A group of children kicked a ball around near a crumbling statue of a man on a horse, probably the town's founder or someone equally significant.

"It's quaint." She looked down. The drop was about three and a half meters. "And we can make the jump if we have to get out this way."

He studied her. "Do you ever switch off?"

She snorted softly. "I try not to. This isn't a holiday. Don't think Markov can't get to you here. We have to be prepared for anything."

"I thought we'd be safe here." He sat down on the edge of the bed, which creaked under his weight. "Nobody knows where we are, right?"

"Maybe, but we need contingencies, just in case." Always be prepared—that was the motto that had been drummed into her during her training.

"Okay. Well, you come up with the contingencies. I'm going to take a shower." Damian bent over and unzipped his backpack. "Unless you want to go first?"

She shook her head. "Go ahead. I'm going to take a look around before it gets too crowded. I need to check out a few things."

He frowned. "You're going to leave me here alone?"

"Yeah, but you'll be fine. I'm going to lock you in since we only have one key."

"You could leave the key with me," he suggested. "I'll let you in when you get back."

Thorn hesitated. "I'd prefer to keep it with me."

His expression darkened. "Don't you trust me to stay put?"

"Of course," she lied. "I just think it's safer this way."

The muscles in his jaw tensed. "Fine. You're the boss."

Damian stripped off his T-shirt, and Thorn left with the image of his finely tuned torso burned into her retina.

CHAPTER 14

*T*horn set off, map in hand, cursing under her breath. Why did Damian have to be so goddamn well put together? Why couldn't he be a geek, like computer nerds were supposed to be? Then she wouldn't be having this problem.

But no, instead, she was stuck with a man who looked like he'd stepped out of a Calvin Klein ad. Damian, standing in his bedroom, in that tiny towel.

His body wet and glistening, muscles rippling beneath his bronzed skin.

And those eyes—dark, stormy, and filled with something that made her stomach flip every time they met hers.

Dammit.

Her freakin' hormones were buzzing again, a low hum that made it impossible to focus on anything else. She sucked in a breath of warm, dry air, trying to clear her head.

Concentrate.

But it was no use. The memory of his body was branded into her mind, every hard line and defined muscle. The way the water had clung to him, dripping down his chest, tracing the contours of his abs, had her insides tightening in a way that was completely unprofessional.

Putting Damian's chiseled physique firmly out of her mind was a losing battle, but she tried, burying the image deep. She studied the map, forcing herself to focus. Any apps on her phone were useless here, thanks to the poor reception, so they were going "old school." She examined the layout of the village, noting it wasn't very big.

Next, she took a walk around their hotel. It was situated between two other buildings. On one side was an old residence with subdivided apartments, and on the other, a farmacia, with what she assumed were the drugstore's lodgings upstairs.

There was no access to the hotel from the sides, even though a narrow alleyway separated it from each of its neighbors. At the front was the big wooden door they'd come through, while at the back, facing the square, was a smaller door leading to a tiled patio with a round table and several chairs.

Two points of entry.

Thorn pushed open the smaller door and found herself in a rustic dining room. Their hostess, along with a younger woman, was setting the tables for breakfast.

"Hola," Thorn smiled. At least she knew how to say hello. In her defense, she had spent the last five years in the Middle East. Her Pashto was far better than her Spanish.

The younger woman glanced up. "Hola, you are staying at the hotel?"

"You speak English," Thorn said, relieved.

"Sí. I'm Clara, Isabella's niece."

"Hi, Clara, it's great to meet you."

"You want breakfast?" Clara gestured to the table settings.

"Not right now. I'm going for a walk."

She nodded. "You come when you want."

Thorn walked through the plaza, scouting out the various shops and cafes. The kids were still playing their soccer game and gave her toothy grins and waves as she passed. She waved back.

On the far side of the plaza, she came across yet another alleyway. It ran between a coffee shop and a grocery store. Thorn glanced around, then followed it for a quarter mile before emerging on a quiet, suburban street flanked by residences. Some were subdivided, but most were free-standing houses.

She consulted the map, looking for an escape route. If things went south, she wanted to be prepared. If she turned right here and walked roughly three hundred yards along the quiet street, then turned left, passing what looked like a park or children's playfield, she'd end up on a main road heading out of town.

Only one way to find out.

She took off at a jog, following the route in her head. Once she turned off the suburban road, the terrain became dry and dusty, the track flanked by a few trees and dried-out bushes. The few properties she saw were set back from the path and behind high walls. Either this was a rich part of town or very poor; she couldn't decide which.

The walls, made of stone and concrete, needed painting, but that meant nothing. There could have been sprawling mansions behind them or small, dilapidated houses.

As she ran past, a wooden gate groaned open, and a teenage boy stepped out. He wore jeans and a T-shirt, and his shoes were faded and smudged with dirt. Thorn came to a stop and gave him a friendly smile. "Hola."

He gave a shy nod, then hurried away. She noticed he carried a woven bag under one arm, and she guessed he was going to the market square to buy groceries.

On a whim, she climbed the wooden gate he'd come

through and glanced over the top. It was a sprawling complex of low-income housing, fronted by a dried-grass area that had been turned into a makeshift basketball court. Several kids the same age as the boy played on it, some barefoot, others in flip-flops, and a few in trainers.

Thorn dropped back onto the path. Nothing of use there.

She walked to the end of the track where it opened up into another, smaller square. This one had a big oak tree in the middle, surrounded by a bench. It seemed to be a pedestrian-only plaza, as there were no cars. Two old ladies sat on the bench chatting.

Five four or five at the most. Late seventies.

Zero threat.

Thorn nodded as she walked past, and they gazed at her with undisguised curiosity.

Two roads led off the square. Inspecting the map, she ascertained that the one on the right joined up with the main road leading out of town. The one on the left led to more houses, eventually petering out.

She took one last look around the square, noting the weathered facades of the houses and the small store that looked like it hadn't opened in years. The front was boarded up, and a rusted sign creaked in the breeze.

She sighed, knowing she needed to get back to the hotel, but also dreading it. Because Damian would be there. With his penetrating gaze, his infuriating smirk, and that stupidly perfect body.

Just a job. He's just a job.

But she knew that was a lie, a pitiful attempt to keep the fire inside her from burning out of control.

Satisfied with her reconnaissance, Thorn turned on her heel and broke into a jog, pushing herself harder than necessary, as if the physical exertion could somehow burn away the heat simmering inside her. She tried to focus on the terrain, on the rhythm of her breathing, on anything but the images of Damian that kept flashing through her mind. But no matter how fast she ran, she couldn't outrun the thought of him—waiting for her back at the hotel, half-naked, his eyes dark with that infuriating mix of challenge and desire.

CHAPTER 15

"What did you really do this morning?" Damian's gaze flicked to Thorn as she sat across from him. She'd been gone for over an hour, leaving him to stew in his own frustration. After his shower, there was nothing else to do. No laptop to work on, no internet, and not even his damn cell phone.

He'd paced the small room like a caged animal, his mood darkening with each passing minute.

"I told you, I went for a run." Her voice was steady, but it didn't do much to calm the storm brewing inside him.

He didn't respond immediately, taking in the way her cheeks were flushed from the exercise, her hair slightly tousled from the wind. She looked so damn sexy, and it was driving him crazy. He had to physically restrain himself from reaching across the table, grabbing her, and pulling her against him. Even now, with the sun casting playful shadows in her hair, she took his breath away. But it didn't matter. She'd made it clear she wasn't interested.

It was like a switch had been flipped. The woman who'd kissed him like she was starving for him had turned cold, distant. A perfect professional mask. It was going to be a long, torturous week.

"Okay, while I was out, I scouted the town," she admitted, reaching for her coffee. "In case we have to leave in a hurry."

He arched an eyebrow, trying to tamp down the frustration gnawing at him. "You found us an escape route?"

"Actually, yeah. I think so. We're pretty isolated here. There's only one main road that goes over the mountain, and most of the access roads lead to that."

He nodded, though his thoughts were still on her, still on how close she'd been to him last night. "What are we going to do here for a week if you won't let me go out?"

She frowned, and he could see the wall she was putting up between them. "I didn't say you couldn't go out. That was a one-off. I had to know you were safe."

He couldn't hold back his frustration any longer. "I'm a big boy, Thorn. I can look after myself for an hour. I don't need to be locked into a goddamn hotel bedroom like a child."

Her expression hardened, a defensive shield snapping into place. "It was for your own safety."

"Bullshit. You just don't trust me."

Before she could respond, Clara, a younger version of their hostess, approached with a fruit salad, bread, cheese, and more coffee.

Damian sat back, trying to rein in his temper, but his stomach chose that moment to remind him that they hadn't eaten since the previous day. The growl from his belly was loud enough for Thorn to hear.

"This looks great, Clara," Thorn said, her tone deliberately casual.

Damian glanced at her in surprise. "How do you know her name?" Then it clicked. "Oh, right. You met her this morning."

Thorn didn't reply, but he could see the calmness she was trying to project, and it only irritated him more.

"What's got into you?" Thorn asked after a long, tense pause.

He took a deep, steadying breath, trying to control the growl in his voice. "Nothing. I'm just hungry."

She shot him a look that said, "Really?"

He turned to face her fully, leaning in slightly. "Okay, if you must know, I'm really fucking confused. One minute, we're all over each other, and the next, you turn into an ice queen. I thought we had something. I thought that kiss meant something."

"I explained that," she said icily, though her voice wavered ever so slightly. God, he wished the sun wouldn't play those tricks with her hair. The copper tones danced like fire in the beams of light, and he could barely keep himself from reaching out.

"No, I don't think you did, otherwise I wouldn't be sitting here wondering what the hell I've done wrong."

She sighed, but it didn't soften the tension between them. "You've done nothing wrong. It's all me. This is all my fault. I'm the one who crossed the line. Right from the start, I've let my emotions get in the way of this assignment. It was unprofessional, and I apologize."

"You apologize?" He couldn't hide his shock. How could she be so detached about the whole thing? "That's it?"

She shrugged, her gaze hardening. "I don't know what else you want me to say."

"I want you to be a goddamn human being and acknowledge there was something between us. I want that sassy, fiery, passionate woman back."

"That's not who I am," she hissed, leaning over the table, her eyes blazing with anger and something deeper, something she was trying to suppress.

"That's where you're wrong," he challenged her, his voice low, almost a growl. "That's exactly who you are. You've just chosen to suppress it under layers of official bullshit. Undercover agent?" He laughed bitterly. "That's just an excuse so you don't have to be yourself."

Her eyes flashed with anger. "Don't presume to know me, Damian."

"I know when you're lying to me."

"Is everything okay?" Clara appeared at their table, and Damian had to physically lean back to calm himself down.

Thorn cleared her throat, quickly masking the tension between them. "Yes, everything is great, thanks, Clara."

Clara hesitated, glancing between them before offering a polite smile. "Tomorrow is market day. You can buy lots of nice things in the square. Also, the church at the top of the hill is very nice. You must go and see for yourself."

"We will," Thorn replied smoothly. "Thank you."

Clara nodded and hurried away, leaving an oppressive silence between them.

Damian tried to eat, but the hunger that had gnawed at him moments ago was replaced by something darker, something more primal. Thorn was driving him crazy, and not just with her mixed signals. It was her, the way she moved, the way she looked at him, the way she tried so damn hard to keep that wall between them.

Eventually, Thorn looked across at him, her voice more measured. "We could hike up to the monastery. I saw it on the map."

He stared at her, his anger and desire churning inside him. What he really wanted to do was drag her upstairs, show her just how wrong she was, kiss her until she couldn't remember her own name, let alone her excuses.

Shit.

He exhaled, trying to push the thought from his mind. If

he kept on like this, he might actually act on it, and that would ruin everything.

"That is, if you want to," she added, her tone softening slightly. "We're supposed to be backpackers, so it wouldn't be that strange if we explored the area."

It was a peace offering, of sorts, but it did nothing to ease the tension thrumming between them.

He nodded stiffly, forcing himself to keep his tone neutral. "Yeah. Sounds good."

"Okay, then."

He grunted, turning back to his meal, so she couldn't see the desire in his eyes.

CHAPTER 16

Thorn breathed in the fresh mountain air, taking in the dramatic landscape dotted with hardy shrubs and towering cacti. The vast expanse felt liberating after all the time spent cooped up indoors, but it did nothing to calm the storm raging inside her.

They didn't talk much, but words weren't necessary. The sounds of nature surrounded them—a chorus of birds, the rustling of dry grasses, the occasional flutter of a lizard darting through the underbrush. The sky was a brilliant blue, only a few wisps of white clouds marring its perfection. It would have been idyllic if not for the tension that crackled between them like a live wire.

Every few moments, Thorn looked over her shoulder, her nerves on high alert. Out here, they were exposed, vulnerable. But after Damian's pent-up frustration at breakfast, she knew they needed to do something—anything—to release the pressure building between them.

"There's nobody behind us," Damian called, stopping up ahead. They'd been walking for nearly an hour, scaling the foothills surrounding the town. So far, they hadn't seen another soul.

Thorn forced herself to relax, though it felt futile. This wasn't Colombia. There weren't rebels hiding in the mountains, armed with AK-47s waiting to take them out. But the way her heart raced at the sight of Damian, the way her pulse quickened every time he glanced her way, it was as if she was in the middle of a war zone all over again—only this time, the battle was within.

"I used to go hiking as a kid," Damian said, almost to himself, breaking the silence. "It was a way to escape. I joined a local hiking group, and we'd walk for hours. Sometimes, I even slept out in the mountains. I loved the outdoors."

The wistfulness in his voice tugged at her, a reminder of the boy he'd once been. A boy who'd had to grow up too fast, unlike her, who'd been loved and protected. She bit her lip, fighting the urge to reach out to him, to touch him.

"Our guide taught us about wildflowers and plants. He was a botanist, I think. I can't really remember, but he'd point out the different species to us along the way."

"He sounds nice." Thorn's voice was softer than she intended, betraying the emotions she was trying to suppress.

Damian nodded, a shadow of a smile touching his lips. "He was."

He wandered over to a cluster of bright red flowers growing in the crevice of a rocky outcrop. "Take these, for example."

Thorn followed him, her heart thudding in her chest for reasons that had nothing to do with their surroundings.

"They're called firecracker plants. Hummingbirds love them. They're native to this region."

"Good name." The vibrant red petals were striking against the rugged backdrop.

"They remind me of you," Damian said, his voice dropping to a husky whisper.

Thorn's breath caught. She knew she should stop him, but she couldn't. She was rooted to the spot, his words sinking deep, far too deep.

"Beautiful, resilient, and built to withstand the toughest conditions. Hardy and untouchable. Hiding in the cracks, making it hard for anyone to get close."

Her heart twisted painfully. "I think the fresh air has gone to your head."

But she knew he wasn't just talking about the flowers. He was talking about her, and it was tearing her apart. She couldn't do this. Not here, not now. Her resolve was slipping, and she didn't trust herself to keep it together much longer. "We should keep moving."

She started to walk away, but Damian grabbed her arm, spinning her around to face him. The intensity in his eyes stole her breath.

"Goddammit, Thorn. Did it really mean nothing to you?"

"Nothing," she lied, her voice cracking as she dropped her gaze.

"Liar," he growled, pulling her closer, his grip firm but not harsh. He was daring her to deny the pull between them, to deny the raw, electric attraction that had been building from the moment they'd met.

She shook her head, her voice a mere whisper. "Damian, we can't. Not here. It's too dangerous."

"Trust me, Thorn. It's going to be a lot more dangerous if you don't kiss me right now."

His words hung between them, heavy with the promise of something she was terrified to give in to. She wanted to laugh it off, to brush it aside like she always did, but the way he was looking at her—like he was a man on the edge, ready to jump—it was unraveling her.

His eyes were burning into her, seeing past every wall she'd put up, every defense she'd constructed. He knew. He'd always known.

"Look at me, Thorn."

She was powerless to resist, her gaze lifting to meet his.

That was all it took. In one swift motion, he closed the distance between them, crushing his lips against hers. The kiss was fierce, demanding, with a desperation that sent a shiver of raw need through her. His teeth grazed her lips as his tongue claimed her mouth, hard and possessive, leaving no room for doubt, no room for her to retreat.

She kissed him back with everything she had, the barriers she'd so carefully erected crumbling to dust. There was no going back from this. He was claiming her, and she was letting him.

Her attempt to keep him at bay had failed spectacularly. He'd broken through her defenses, tearing down every last one until she was laid bare, vulnerable, exposed.

And she was unprepared for the torrent of emotions that her surrender unleashed.

A sob caught in her throat, but Damian swallowed the sound, his arms wrapping around her like a shield, protecting her from the storm she'd kept bottled up for so long.

His hands gripped her ass, pulling her flush against him, his need evident in the hard line of his body. He wanted her —God, how he wanted her. And she wanted him just as fiercely, the intensity of it leaving her breathless, disoriented.

Fire raged through her veins, incinerating every thought, every hesitation. How had she ever thought she could walk away from this? From him?

Their attraction was too intense, too primal to ignore. It was a force of nature, undeniable and unstoppable, and she was caught in its grip, powerless to fight it.

She clung to him, her fingers tangling in his hair, needing to feel every inch of him, to burn herself into his memory, just as he was searing himself into hers. She was melting in his embrace, the heat between them scorching her from the inside out.

A desperate moan escaped her lips, a sound she didn't recognize as her own. She was losing herself in him, in this moment, and she didn't care.

Damian pulled back, breaking the kiss with a low, animalistic growl, his chest heaving as he looked down at her, his eyes molten silver, filled with an intensity that left her reeling.

"Now tell me that meant nothing."

THORN COULDN'T REMEMBER WALKING down the mountain. The journey back to the hotel was a blur, the winding alleyways a vague memory. She didn't recall stepping into the cold shower, scrubbing off the sweat, the dirt, and the raw, unbridled lust that had built up during their hike.

It was only when she emerged, shivering and dazed, that her brain cleared just enough to process what had happened.

Okay, so he'd proved his point.

Big deal.

It still didn't mean they should be involved.

If anything, it proved her point—that she couldn't do her job when her mind was so consumed by him. Take the last hour, for example. They could have been ambushed by bandits, blown up by rebels, or attacked by wild animals on the way down the mountain, and she wouldn't have noticed.

He'd left her shattered and shaking, torn up inside. The fire he'd ignited hadn't simply gone out; instead, it burned like a hot, glowing coal, leaving her sweaty, frustrated, and more than a little aroused.

Damn, Damian.

When they'd gotten back, he'd left her alone to grab a pack of beers from the store. She'd let him go, desperately needing the time to regroup, to try to make sense of what had happened out there.

The ice-cold shower had calmed her down, given her some perspective. This had to stop. But how was she going to tell him he couldn't manhandle her like that—even if it was to prove a point? Damian wasn't the type of man to take no for an answer.

That smug look on his handsome face hadn't helped either. It had only made her madder, more frustrated.

By the time he got back from the store, she'd regained some of her composure. "Damian, we need to talk."

Instead of answering, he handed her a wrapped parcel. "I got you something."

Trust him to throw her completely off balance.

She stared at the package. "You got me a gift?"

He grinned, his eyes crinkling at the corners, looking for all the world like a pleased little boy who'd done something clever. Why did that tug at her heartstrings? "It's more of a disguise than a gift."

Intrigued, she pulled open the wrapping, and out tumbled a knee-length blue dress with a subtle floral pattern. She held it up, the fabric flowing over her hands. It was off the shoulder, cinched at the waist, then flared out to her knees.

"It's gorgeous," she said hesitantly, not wanting to appear ungrateful. "But I'm not sure it's me."

"I've seen you in your wedding dress, remember?"

Damn. She had loved the feel of the silk on her skin, the way it swished around her legs. She hated that he knew that, that he had her all figured out.

How?

She hadn't shown him any more of herself than she had

others, yet he'd read her like an open book, like one of his crypto programs. Now he was pressing her buttons, making her do things, feel things, that she never normally would.

This had to stop.

"It'll help you blend in," he said, peeling off his shirt.

Oh, God.

Why did she want to run her hands over his chest so badly? To lose herself in the smell, the taste, the feel of him? She gulped down the urge.

She had to put an end to this… this madness.

Putting down the dress, she said, "Damian, I think we'd better talk about what happened."

"So now you want to talk?" He winked at her, teasing. It made her heart do an odd flip-flop. Since when did they have this light-hearted banter?

At her exasperated look, he relented. "Okay, sure. Let me have a shower, and I'll meet you downstairs. Clara recommended a great little place where we can get dinner."

Nooo! The thought of going out to dinner with him was too much. It wasn't a date. He was making this sound like a vacation.

"We're supposed to be hiding out," she gritted out, trying desperately not to look at his bronzed chest, those toned muscles on display. He might not be as bulky as the SEALs she'd worked with, but he had clear-cut definition, and a six-pack that she wanted to run her tongue over.

Holy hell, what had gotten into her?

"I know, but there's no law that says we can't have fun in the process."

She frowned. Fun equaled distraction equaled danger.

"It's on the other side of the square." He spread his arms wide. "We've got to eat."

That was true.

If they didn't go there, they'd have to go somewhere else,

so they may as well try the restaurant Clara had recommended.

"Okay, sure," she relented, turning her back on him before he could peel off his jeans. That would be a step too far. Having felt his hardness against her on the trail, she didn't think she could handle seeing it in the flesh.

"I won't be long," he said, and she heard the bathroom door click shut.

Exhaling, Thorn eyed the dress lying on the bed.

Should she?

Outside, the sky was deepening into a rich, unrelenting blue, and while the sun still shone brightly, it wasn't as high as it had been.

Would it be so wrong to put it on? It was pretty, and it would feel good against her skin. Her jeans were dusty and worn, her T-shirt still fresh, but she could save it for another day. It would save doing laundry.

Just one day, she whispered to herself. I'll give myself one day to be a normal woman.

It seemed safe enough here in the mountain village. So far, she'd seen nothing out of the ordinary. Nothing that raised alarms.

But twenty-four hours was all she was going to compromise on. Then she'd snap back to reality. This craziness could not be allowed to continue. She was a former Special Agent, for heaven's sake, and she had a job to do. Not even that silver-eyed devil would prevent her from doing it.

Decision made, she picked up the dress.

CHAPTER 17

*D*amian walked into the empty breakfast room that doubled as a waiting area, and his breath caught in his throat.

Fucking hell, she was gorgeous.

Heat spread through him, rendering the cold shower he'd taken earlier useless. "I knew it would look good on you."

She did a half turn, her eyes shining. "It's very pretty. Thank you."

The only problem was that every goddamned man in the place would be staring at her. If he'd wanted them to blend in, he'd made a colossal mistake. With her copper hair and pale skin, she was already a knockout, but now, in that dress —floral swirls and soft chiffon clinging to her every curve— she was absolutely stunning.

At least the attention wouldn't be on him for once.

They walked across the plaza, absorbing the evening sounds. A group of teenagers lounged by the fountain, laughing and joking, while locals hurried home after a long day at work. "Clara said this place opens early and closes at ten," he told Thorn.

"Sounds great." Her smile made his heart lurch in his chest. He hardly recognized her now. She actually looked like she was having fun. They still had to talk—he knew that—but he wasn't in any rush to end this brief respite between them.

He wasn't a fool. He knew what she wanted to discuss, and she was totally justified. This insane attraction between them was throwing her off her game. He knew it, and she knew it. Thorn had lost her prickles, transformed into a beautiful Rose, but that meant she was vulnerable. And if she was vulnerable, he was vulnerable too.

Without her full attention, they were both at risk—as was his presence at CryptoCon, and the update the FBI so desperately needed him to implement.

For a crazy moment, he considered asking her to run away with him. Leave all this behind. Let the bad guys win this round. The FBI could hunt down Markov later.

At least they would be free.

He had enough money to support them both. It wasn't a completely unrealistic fantasy.

Except, he knew she wouldn't go for it. No way. Not Thorn.

She was too principled, too committed. Too proud to rely on him, no matter what he made her feel. He might have forced her to admit she had feelings for him, but she wasn't about to give up her job, her independence, and her livelihood to follow him into the sunset.

Without this crypto update, he was just a common criminal.

The FBI would come after him for his past sins. They'd only agreed to wipe his record clean on the understanding that he'd help them bring down a whole bunch of bad guys, including the most notorious arms dealer in America.

That deal still stood.

He sighed, then glanced at Thorn, who was absorbing the sights and sounds of the plaza, a peaceful look on her face that he hadn't seen before.

Maybe all they were going to get were snippets of calm, in which case, he was determined to enjoy it before it was gone again, and real life intruded.

The restaurant Clara had suggested was a simple, rustic taverna tucked away in a narrow alley on the far side of the plaza. The wooden door, set back in an alcove, was easy to miss during the day when shadows obscured the decorative tile bearing the restaurant's name.

"After you," Damian said, holding the door open.

Thorn stepped inside and uttered a soft, "Wow."

Damian looked around. The cozy taverna was already half full. Diners were laughing and drinking, while music played softly in the background. The smell of garlic filled the air, but it wasn't overwhelming thanks to the open patio door on the far side that led out to a pretty courtyard bursting with pink bougainvillea.

"Buena noches." The maître d' came over to greet them.

Damian asked for their table.

At Thorn's quizzical look, he said, "I made a reservation, but don't worry, I didn't give my real name."

"You've thought of everything." She shot him a sly look.

He had. He wanted this to be special—a small piece of normalcy in the madness that had overtaken his life.

The waiter led them to a table for two at the back, close to the courtyard. A soft breeze took the edge off the heat.

"This is perfect." Thorn gave him a hesitant smile as she sat down.

He loved making her face light up like that. The way her green eyes sparkled… It stroked his ego, stroked other parts of his body too.

Shit, he had it bad.

Doug would say he was smitten. His friend had often asked if he'd felt that way about Christine, but when he'd said he hadn't, Doug had let it slide.

Then again, Thorn was a beautiful, complicated, intriguing woman. Of course he'd be lusting after her. Any red-blooded man would, right?

Except in the back of his mind, he feared it was more than that. She'd gotten under his skin, and he couldn't stop thinking about how she'd responded to his kiss, about what he'd like to do to her to make those eyes really shine.

The waiter came back with a jug of sangria and two glasses. Before Thorn had a chance to object, he'd poured them each a glass.

"I'm sure one won't hurt." Damian held it up. "Cheers."

She eyed him across the table. "Maybe just the one. What should we drink to?"

"How about living in the moment?" He fixed his gaze on her.

She tilted her head. "Good one."

For some reason, those two little words filled him with joy. She was his, if only for this moment.

They ordered carnitas tacos with a side of refried beans and arroz con pollo, a classic chicken and rice dish seasoned with saffron and peppers. It was insanely delicious. They were ordering coffee when a rakishly handsome Spaniard with long hair in a leather jacket carrying a guitar walked into the center of the restaurant.

The crowd, who as far as Damian could tell, hadn't turned over once, applauded and whistled.

"What's happening?" Thorn asked.

The waiter explained and Damian translated for her. "He said Carlos is a flamenco guitarist. He's in town for one night only and is going to perform for us."

From the first strum of Carlos's guitar, the crowd went

quiet. It was as if someone had flipped a switch. Damian shifted his chair around, sliding in next to Thorn, noticing how everyone else seemed to be doing the same. The space was tight, so close their arms almost brushed.

Carlos was good—really good. The kind of good that made you stop whatever you were doing and just listen. He played a sweet, haunting melody, and next to him, Thorn went very quiet.

Damian couldn't tell what was going on in her head, but he noticed how she gulped her water like she was trying to swallow something more than just the liquid. She blinked rapidly, and for a second, he thought he caught a glimmer of tears in her eyes, but before he could be sure, she was already looking away, pretending everything was fine.

The next song picked up the pace. The crowd sat up straighter and began tapping their shoes in time to the music. Carlos was really putting on a show now—his fingers dancing across the strings like they had a life of their own. It was impossible not to get caught up in it.

The song ended and everyone broke into enthusiastic applause, himself included, but Carlos didn't miss a beat. He smiled, revealing a set of perfect teeth, and dove straight into the next number.

This one was different.

It started off slow and smooth, but there was something raw underneath it, something that made the air feel thicker. Damian was suddenly very aware of Thorn sitting beside him. When he leaned over to grab his beer, his arm brushed hers, and he felt a jolt, like static electricity, ripple through him.

Now that had never happened before. Not with Christine, not with anyone.

Carlos was pushing the tempo now, fingers flying over the guitar in a way that seemed almost impossible. The room felt like it was holding its breath, everyone on the edge of their seats, himself included, waiting for the final note.

And when it came, Carlos ended with a dramatic sweep of his hand, leaving the audience in stunned silence before they erupted into cheers.

Damian turned to Thorn. He didn't know about anyone else, but he was fully aroused. Painfully so. Flushed, with her coppery hair tumbling around her face, and those huge emerald eyes glowing softly, luring him in, Thorn had never looked more enticing.

The air was thick with unresolved tension.

"Damian, I—" She stopped, searching for the right thing to say.

But there were no words for this.

He took her hand and leaned forward, his voice rougher than he'd intended. "Let's get the check."

CHAPTER 18

Thorn was a hot, sweaty mess when they left the taverna, but once they'd gotten back to the hotel, she was beyond salvaging. Too far gone to even consider objecting, she let Damian lead her by the hand up to their room.

As soon as Damian kicked the door shut, they collided like magnets. His arms encircled her back, trapping her against him, while she lifted her chin, already seeking out his mouth.

With a groan, he lowered his head and claimed her lips, kissing her deep and hard until her head was spinning.

Oh, God.

She was swirling out of control. The rush was all-consuming, and any semblance of rational thought flew from her mind as his lips crushed against hers, bruising in their intensity.

His hot tongue delved into her mouth, probing, exploring, devouring.

She was burning up inside. The taste of him, his masculine scent, his aftershave—so intense, so addictive—it was all too much. She was losing it.

Melting.

Incinerating.

It was crazy, yet somehow, she craved more. Clutching onto his arms, she kissed him back fiercely, hearing him growl. His hands became more urgent, running up her back, tugging the dress off her shoulders.

No argument there.

One day...

One day to give in to the desire that had been raging through her since they'd first met. That messed up emotion that had skewed her opinion of him, the revelation about righting wrongs, the naked attraction she couldn't ignore—it all came out now in this deep, toe-curling kiss.

"Damian..." she gasped, as his mouth moved from her lips to her neck, and down to her shoulder. His stubble burned a scorching trail across her skin, making her tilt her neck back to give him better access.

He paused, looking up at her. His fiery gaze filled with such heat, it made her legs weak. There was a question in his eyes, as if he were giving her a chance to resist, a chance to push him away.

She didn't.

If she were honest, she'd known this would happen from the moment he'd given her the blue dress. Possibly even earlier, from the kiss on the mountain trail.

One night...

A triumphant glimmer lit his eyes as he tugged the dress down until it was bunched around her waist. Her breasts jumped free, the sports bra doing nothing to stop her nipples from hardening into tight little buds.

In one quick move, he unsnapped the fastens at the back, and it flew off, exposing her bare breasts. Now she was totally exposed, but she didn't care. Not when she saw the look on his face. Awe, mixed with something much more intense.

He emitted another low groan as he sucked a nipple into his mouth.

The heat.

His mouth was scorching hot, and she cried out as his tongue caressed the engorged nub. Her breasts hadn't been touched, other than by her own hand, for nearly a decade. They weren't used to this type of searing onslaught.

Sparks flew from her breasts to her belly, to her core, and she clamped her legs together as she felt a surge of wetness.

"Relax," he murmured, his mouth moving to the other breast. "Let yourself enjoy it."

Oh, God. She was going to self-combust. Any moment now and she'd burst into flames. It was too much, too overwhelming.

A sob escaped her, and he glanced up. "It's okay, we'll take it slow."

Slow?

Who was he kidding?

She was an inferno burning from the inside out. A raging, out-of-control wildfire.

He straightened up and reclaimed her mouth. His kiss was gentler this time, but no less scorching. If anything, it seared deeper, caressing her mouth, making her feel things she hadn't felt in years.

It drew her out, slowly but surely, probing into her soul. Her nipples tingled from his tongue, wet and on fire. Her body cried out for more, yet the words didn't come.

Still, he knew.

She didn't have to say anything, her body was saying it for her.

He peeled her dress the rest of the way off, letting it drop around her ankles. The look in his eyes as he gazed at her nakedness was enough to make her melt into a puddle of longing, right then and there.

"Christ, Rose, you're beautiful."

Picking her up, he laid her on the bed, then covered her with his body. They kissed again, deep and searing, until she was weak with longing. She clawed at his back, pinning him close, wanting to feel as much of him as possible, in case this spell suddenly broke.

Then suddenly, his mouth was burning a trail to her breasts, capturing them one by one, turning them from cool to scorching hot in the blink of an eye. She gasped, arching her back, the sensation was so exquisite.

How could anything feel this good? A tightly coiled tension began to build in her stomach, growing as he sucked and flicked at her nipples with his tongue. Just when she thought she couldn't stand it anymore, he stopped, releasing her breast. Her entire body was buzzing with something she couldn't describe.

It was crazy, insane, intense—and she loved it.

He was kissing her stomach now, his tongue delving into her belly button, making her squirm. Every nerve ending was on fire, her body overly sensitive.

She shuddered as he pulled down her soaked panties, sliding the material over her skin. She was past caring. Moaning, she lifted her hips, barely conscious of what she was doing. All she knew was she needed to get some release. Somehow.

"Please," she begged, as he ran a hand down her leg, his other resting on her stomach, just above her pubic hair. He stroked her gently, his hand moving further down until his thumb pressed between her slick folds, making her gasp.

With mesmerizing slowness, he began to rotate his finger in small circles over her clit, until she was writhing with wild abandon. If this was what it felt like to be normal, she wanted more of it. Much more.

A whole army of drones could drop bombs on the hotel, and she wouldn't notice.

"Damian," she hissed, grasping the bed covers, her hands balling into fists. But instead of replying, he bent his head and his tongue took the place of his finger.

Thorn cried out, letting go of the sheet and clutching his head. Fire burst through her, exploding upwards until her whole body was trembling. He sucked at her core, his teeth grazing her, sending shockwaves of pure desire through her already shaking body.

His big hands moved to her hips, pressing down, anchoring her so he could have his full. His mouth ravaged her, until she was a dripping, yelping mess.

Thorn wasn't sure how much more she could stand. A sob wracked her body, as she gasped his name. He sucked hard, drawing her clit into his mouth.

Fuuuck.

She couldn't handle it anymore. She was right on the edge. The tightness in her stomach grew, until she was wound so tightly she felt like she was going to unleash at any moment. She was soaring, flying higher and higher, swirling into nothingness.

One last suck and she was flying off the edge of the cliff, crying out as spasm after spasm consumed her body. She bucked like a woman possessed, but he moved with her, letting her ride it out, his mouth still attached like a limpet.

She came so hard, she saw stars. Over and over again, smaller convulsions spread through her, until she was totally and utterly spent. Only then did he break their bond.

Exhausted and more than a little hazy, she collapsed back on the bed, her eyes closed. It was only then that she remembered he'd called her Rose.

* * *

Damian watched as she collapsed, utterly spent on the bed, her beautiful body still trembling with aftershocks. Her breath came in shallow, rapid bursts, her chest rising and falling like she'd just run a marathon.

Fuck, she fired his blood.

His cock strained against his jeans, throbbing with unfulfilled desire. If he didn't get inside her soon, he was going to explode.

As she recovered, he stripped off his clothes, letting them fall to the floor. The bed creaked as he crawled onto it, making her eyes flutter open.

"Damian, that was…" She gave a shy smile. "Wow."

Her flushed skin, the way her eyes shone when she gazed at him, and that soft, vulnerable expression on her face—hell, he wanted her so bad.

"That was the warmup," he said, his voice low and throaty. Her eyes dropped to his cock and widened. What he saw there nearly sent him over the edge. No fear, no apprehension, just a quick gasp and a silent invitation. Heat surged through his body, the need almost too great to handle.

She grabbed at him as he collapsed on top of her, their bodies slamming together. His mouth hungrily found hers, as her legs wrapped around his waist, drawing him close.

He positioned himself at her opening and slid inside her. She was wet and slick, and so goddamn hot he could barely hang on. It was like nothing he'd ever experienced—intense, raw, and completely consuming.

"Jesus, Thorn…"

She whimpered as he encased himself fully inside her. Holy fucking hell, he was drowning in her tight heat. It was all he could do not to shoot his load right there and then.

He tried to savor the moment of complete connection but

didn't have the control. It was too intense, and he was too thick and swollen, too close to the edge. He withdrew and plunged in again, harder this time, with more force.

She cried out as he buried himself deeper, feeling her soft folds envelop him, absorbing him like they were meant to be together. The perfect fit.

He repeated the motion, knowing he was fucking close to coming, but wanting to prolong the exquisite agony. She moaned as he pounded into her, over and over again, until she was shifting up the bed with every thrust. The headboard slammed against the wall, and her glorious breasts jiggled up and down with the force. Both their bodies were coated with perspiration.

He'd never seen anything more sensual. In this moment, she was totally and fully his.

Time seemed to blur as they moved together, matching thrust for thrust, perfectly in sync. He plunged so fucking deep that he worried he'd split her in two.

Her cries escalated until her orgasm hit. Her body convulsed, lifting high off the bed like a woman possessed. Her head tilted back as spasms rocked her body.

Her sudden tightness sent him flying over the edge. A groan tore from his throat, his entire body shaking as he let go. And then he was coming deep inside her.

Like a pressure valve had blown off, he emptied his hot seed inside her, over and over again, until he had nothing left to give.

CHAPTER 19

The piercing scream cut through the silence like a bullet, yanking Thorn out of the deepest sleep she'd had in days. Adrenaline flooded her system, pushing away the fog of exhaustion. Damian had made her reach heights she'd never dreamed of, never even knew were possible, but now that was the furthest thing from her mind.

She reached instinctively for the Glock under her pillow, the cold metal familiar and comforting in her grip. Her mind snapped into focus, heart pounding in her chest as she scanned the room, senses on high alert.

Damian lay naked beside her, his chest rising and falling steadily. He hadn't stirred, hadn't heard the scream, and was blissfully unaware of the danger that might be closing in on them.

Had she imagined it?

Had it been another nightmare, another ghost from her past?

But the hair on the back of her neck prickled, an old instinct warning her that something was off. Years of training told her to trust that feeling.

She peeled back the comforter and slid silently out of bed. The room was dim, the only light coming from the sliver of moonlight slipping through the partially open blinds. Thorn pressed her ear to the door, holding her breath as she listened.

The low murmur of a man's voice drifted up the stairs, deep and menacing. It was followed by the shaky, high-pitched response of a woman. Thorn's jaw clenched. Fear was thick in the woman's voice—Isabella.

Definitely trouble.

Moving quickly, Thorn pulled on her leggings and T-shirt with the efficiency of someone who had done this too many times to count. She unlocked the door and edged her way to the top of the stairs, her body pressed close to the wall, out of sight. The voices became clearer as she crept forward.

"¿Has visto a este hombre?"

She knew enough Spanish to understand: Have you seen this man?

"No, no lo he visto." Isabella's voice trembled, but she lied with conviction.

Damn it.

This was bad—worse than she'd anticipated.

Who the hell had tracked them down?

Alek Markov?

Her mind raced through the possibilities as she leaned over the railing to get a better look. In the dim light of the foyer, she spotted them. Two men—big, dangerous, and armed.

The first one had a knife to Isabella's throat, his grip on the blade confident and too smooth. His build was massive, over six feet tall and pushing three hundred pounds, with the kind of bulk that suggested military training—maybe a mercenary. The way he moved told her he was experienced, deadly.

The second man, shorter but still built like a tank, was holding up a photo—likely of Damian.

Threat level: lethal.

They were professionals, hired muscle with no qualms about getting their hands dirty. Thorn's pulse quickened as she assessed the situation. One shot in the chamber. Even with her skill, it wasn't enough to take them both out before one of them hurt Isabella. She needed another plan.

She backed away from the railing and returned to the bedroom, her mind already calculating their next move. She locked the door behind her and shook Damian awake, her voice low but urgent. "Damian, get up. We've got to move."

"What?" he mumbled, groggy and disoriented. "Why?"

"They're here. They found us." Her tone left no room for argument.

Damian bolted upright, the gravity of the situation sinking in as his eyes snapped open. "Shit. How?"

"No time for questions. Get dressed and make it fast." Thorn was already stripping the bed, shoving the sheets into the closet to make it look like they hadn't slept there. The less evidence, the better. Isabella was risking her life to protect them, and Thorn wasn't about to let that be in vain.

Damian scrambled to pull on his clothes, his hands a little unsteady as he grabbed his wallet from the bedside table. Thorn didn't stop moving, her mind going through the escape plan in her head. She strapped her knife to her ankle and retrieved a short piece of electrical wire from her backpack, stuffing it down her leggings along with the map.

Damian raised an eyebrow but didn't ask, sensing the urgency in her movements. Now was not the time for explanations.

She tossed her pack into the closet, grabbed the burner phone, then yanked on her running shoes. She couldn't run with a heavy pack, not where they were going. It would slow them down.

Damian, still adjusting to the shock, reached for his backpack, instinctively gathering up items to stash inside it.

Thorn caught his arm. "Leave it. We're out of time."

His eyes widened, but he nodded, hurling the pack in beside hers, then closing the closet door.

Thorn pushed open the window, assessing the drop. It wasn't ideal, but it was doable. "You first."

To his credit, Damian didn't argue. He hurried back to the window, swinging his leg over the balcony railing with more agility than she expected, and dropped softly to the ground.

Thorn followed, pausing only to make sure the window was shut behind them. The shutters were a problem—left open, they might raise suspicion, but there was no time to fix that now. Hopefully, the thugs wouldn't notice.

The drop was significant, but Thorn landed with practiced ease. She crouched as she hit the ground, absorbing the impact and quickly scanning the area. The plaza was empty—no lookout posted. A rookie mistake, but one she'd take full advantage of.

"Follow me," she whispered, moving swiftly across the square toward the dark alleyway, Damian right behind her.

"Where are we going?" he whispered, his voice tight.

Thorn didn't answer immediately, her mind focused on their escape. The night clung to them like a shroud as they darted through the narrow, labyrinthine alleyways. The air was warm and dry, mingled with the faint stench of decay from overflowing dumpsters. Every step they took echoed eerily in the silence, the only sound in a town that was fast asleep.

"Out of town," she finally muttered, her voice low and resolute.

Damian kept pace beside her, his breathing steady, his

footsteps heavier but as sure as hers. Not surprising given his athleticism. It would come in handy now.

They rounded a corner, and Thorn led Damian down a dusty lane lined with scraggly trees. The high wall of a housing complex loomed on their right, its bricks weathered and worn, with a dry, worn-out creeper clinging desperately to the cracks.

She kept her eyes peeled for any sign of movement. The quiet was unnerving, but it also reassured her that they were the only people around.

"This way." She gestured to a narrower path ahead, barely wide enough for two people to walk side by side. The walls on either side seemed to close in on them, the space shrinking as they pressed forward. Thorn could hear Damian behind her. He was keeping up, quick and silent, not asking unnecessary questions.

The path opened up into a small square, the kind that once might have been charming but now lay in neglect. An ancient oak tree stood in the center, its gnarled branches casting twisted shadows on the ground. The wind rustled through the leaves, making the tree groan as if protesting their intrusion.

Thorn's gaze swept across the surrounding buildings, derelict and crumbling, their windows dark and lifeless. She was searching for something. Something she'd seen earlier. An escape.

She spotted it then, a small porch partially hidden by overgrown bushes. Her heartbeat quickened as a plan formed. She peered over a low fence that separated the porch from the square. A motorcycle, barely visible in the gloom, sat in the shadow of the building.

Yes. That would do.

She opened the gate with a low squeak, and they paused, waiting for a light to come on, or a face to appear at the window, but neither happened, so they ventured in, leaving the gate open.

"The motorcycle?" Damian whispered, following her thoughts.

"Yeah. What do you think? Is it usable?" She remembered he had a Harley-Davidson in his garage, so he probably knew a thing or two about motorcycles.

He inspected it, bending down to take a close look. "I think so. It's old, but still in use. I'd say someone rides this regularly. No key, though."

"If we can hotwire it, we can use it." Thorn reached into the waistband of her leggings and pulled out the thin wire.

Damian stared at her. "You know how to do this?"

She bit back a grin. "It's not my first rodeo." Using her knife, she cut a small section of the wire. Damian's eyes widened as he watched her, a mixture of surprise and admiration on his face, as she worked her magic on the ignition connector. There was a brief click, and then the engine hummed to life, the sound barely louder than a whisper.

"Nice," Damian muttered, impressed. He gave the bike a hesitant push, guiding it through the gate to a safe distance, before fully engaging the engine. The low rumble vibrated through the square. A light went on in the house.

Thorn had expected as much. "Let's go," she hissed, urgently.

Damian swung his leg over the seat and grasped the handlebars. Adjusting the controls, he whispered, "Hop on."

"I take it you're driving?" She couldn't resist the jab. He hadn't even given her the option. She might be his bodyguard, but Damian was definitely an alpha male, and he liked to fulfill that role.

"Hell, yeah."

A face appeared at the window, silhouetted against the

light. They heard frantic knocking, and a muffled shout echoed into the night.

"Time to go," Thorn murmured, jumping on behind him and wrapping her arms around his waist. The warmth of his body was reassuring, and she pushed the intruding memories of their lovemaking firmly from her mind.

Damian revved the engine. "Yes, ma'am."

With a somewhat shaky kick, the bike lurched forward and sped across the square, just as the door opened and a woman came out yelling something indeterminate.

She tightened her grip on Damian, eyes fixed on the road ahead. He maneuvered along the tree-lined streets to the road that led out of town, where they picked up speed.

Thorn didn't relax until the twisted maze of a village was behind them, fading into the distance.

CHAPTER 20

*A*s they roared out of the town, the lights of the small village were replaced by the shadowy embrace of the mountains. The road twisted and climbed, the engine's growl echoing off the sheer rock faces that loomed on either side.

Damian kept his eyes on the road ahead, the moonlight casting eerie shadows that danced across the asphalt. The mountain pass was narrow and treacherous, with steep drops just beyond the guardrails.

It was the only way in or out of the town, a natural bottleneck. His pulse quickened. If they were being pursued, this was where the danger would close in.

Used to handling a motorcycle, he maneuvered around the tight corners with ease, avoiding the loose gravel. The wind whipped through his hair, the chill of the night air cooling his skin.

Despite the situation, it felt good to be on the road again.

Thorn tightened her grip around his waist, and he smiled into the darkness. The fact she was behind him made it even better. The altitude made his ears pop, but he barely noticed, his mind focused on the ride and the woman molded to his back.

It was easy to imagine a different scenario. One where he was free, and she was his woman. They were on vacation, taking a joy ride, just the two of them. Except that fantasy had come to a shattering halt when the two men with guns had burst into their hotel. He'd thought they were safe, but he'd been wrong.

Thank God Thorn had woken up. He hadn't heard a thing.

If it had been a couple of hours earlier, neither of them would have seen it coming. He ground his jaw at the sobering thought.

She was right. Fooling around was distracting, and it put both their lives at risk.

But he was right too. They did have something special, but he knew now that something special would have to wait.

He'd admit that much.

Finally, after what felt like hours of winding through the mountains, they crested the highest point of the pass. The road began its descent, the landscape opening up into a vast expanse of rugged terrain, punctuated by distant peaks that seemed to stretch on forever.

A dusty intersection came into view, illuminated softly by streetlights, and he felt Thorn tap him on the shoulder. He pulled over beneath a weathered signpost and cut the engine. The silence that followed was almost deafening, broken only by the ticking of the cooling engine and the faint rustle of the wind.

"You gonna tell me what happened?" He twisted around in the seat.

Thorn dismounted and marched up and down, stretching her legs—legs that seemed to go on and on in those leggings. She wore trainers but no socks. Neither did he. There'd been no time. "I heard a scream and went to take a look. I saw Isabella with two thugs. One had a knife to her throat."

"Jesus," he hissed. "Was she okay?"

"I hope so. She told them she hadn't seen us, and he seemed to believe her."

"That's why we put everything in the closet?" He was catching on. She hadn't wanted to leave any trace of their stay.

She nodded. "I thought about taking them out, but firstly, I couldn't be sure they wouldn't hurt Isabella or Clara, and secondly, it would confirm we were there. When they didn't check in, whoever sent them would know we were on the run."

"Alek," he hissed.

"Could be. The men spoke Spanish, and they looked like hired mercenaries. Is that something Markov would do?"

His eyes slanted. "Yeah."

She nodded. "What I don't understand is how he found us. We didn't tell anyone where we were going. The only people who knew our location were Anna, Hawk, Pat, and the chopper pilot."

"You think there is a leak?" he asked, frowning.

She gnawed on her lower lip. "I friggin' hope not, otherwise we're in a shitload of trouble."

She could say that again. How the hell were they going to make it to the conference if they didn't know who to trust? He didn't say as much, however, since they were in the middle of nowhere and there was nothing they could do about it right now. The most important thing was to get out of sight.

"Which way?" He glanced up at the signpost. "We'd better not spend too long out in the open." The sign was old, the paint faded, but still readable: one direction pointed back to

Puebla, another toward Veracruz, and the third straight ahead, deeper into the heart of Mexico.

"Let me take a look." Thorn unfolded the map, spreading it out on the seat of the bike. She studied it quickly, and he could see her mind working through their options. "We head straight, toward Mexico City. If they do suspect we were in Las Piedras, they'll expect us to go toward Veracruz or back to Puebla, but I think we should take the opposite route."

Damian rubbed his jaw. "Shouldn't we steer clear of the big cities?"

"We're not going into the city." She traced a route on the map with her finger. "We'll bypass it and head toward the Sierra de Puebla mountains. There's a place I know there, deep in the hills, where we can lay low for a few days, maybe longer if we need to. It's remote—off the grid. I'll call Pat from there and tell him what happened."

He frowned. "Why didn't you mention this place before? We could have gone there instead of Las Piedras."

"It's my parents' place, or rather it was. It's mine now. I didn't want to use it for an op, but now…" She shrugged.

"Now it could save our ass," he finished for her. He was dying to know how her folks had a place out here, but he shelved that question for later. Again, it wasn't the time.

They climbed back on the motorcycle, and he twisted the throttle, enjoying the sound of the engine roaring to life.

As they cruised down the deserted highway, Damian felt the steady thrum of the engine beneath him. It was almost comforting. Thorn's arms were wrapped tightly around his waist, her warmth seeping through the leather of his jacket.

She leaned into him, shielding herself from the biting night wind, and he relished the closeness. For once, they weren't sniping at each other's heads or devouring each other; they were simply enjoying each other's warmth.

The miles melted away under the tires as they navigated the quiet, empty roads. Eventually, they rolled into a forgotten little village tucked into the foothills of the Sierra de Puebla.

The place barely qualified as a town—more like a blink-and-you-miss-it crossroads, with a handful of houses huddled together and a lone gas station that looked like it hadn't seen any real business in years. The pumps were old, their paint chipped and faded, relics from a time that had long since passed.

Damian cut the engine, his eyes gritty from the long ride. "We need gas. Got any cash?"

"Yeah," she said, pulling a wad of pesos from her pocket. He filled up the motorcycle tank while she kept watch. When he was done, she walked toward the small, grimy building where a faint light flickered inside.

As she stepped through the door, Damian held his breath. Through the dusty window, he saw her approach the counter. By the looks of things, the interior appeared just as rundown as the outside.

Even from here, he could see a man slumped behind the counter, half-asleep, his attention fixed on a tiny TV. Thorn placed the cash on the counter, the exchange quick and silent. The man barely looked at her before handing over a crumpled receipt, no questions asked. Thorn had everything under control.

Damian exhaled, the tension in his shoulders easing slightly as she stepped back outside. She tucked the receipt into her pocket as she walked toward him, then gave him a thumbs-up.

"Let's move," she said. "We've still got a way to go."

They continued their journey, leaving the sleepy gas station behind and heading back out onto the open road. According to the map, they were about an hour from Mexico

City, after which they'd need to make a hard turn into the mountains.

Damian knew it would take another two or three hours to reach their destination, a small place called Taxco. Doing the entire trip in one go, and on a motorcycle, was brutal, but it wasn't like they had any better options. The Yamaha wasn't built for speed, but Damian pushed it as hard as he could, the engine straining as they devoured the miles.

They skirted around Mexico City, avoiding the heavy traffic that was starting to build as the first light of dawn crept into the sky. They took every back road and side street they could find, navigating the city's outskirts with a mix of instinct and Thorn's directions. By the time they left the city behind, the sun was starting to rise, casting a warm, golden glow over the surrounding hills.

Once they were in the mountains, Damian pulled over, his eyes gritty and his arms aching from gripping the handlebars. They swapped places, and Thorn drove them the rest of the way.

He knew they were fleeing for their lives, but damned if her ass didn't feel great sandwiched between his thighs. The roar of the engine and the soft bouncing over the mountainous roads left him with a cock harder than the granite hills around them.

Finally, they pulled off the road beside a sprawling farmhouse, surrounded by a wooden fence in desperate need of repair.

"Do your parents still come here?" he asked, masking his erection by studying the outside of the property.

"No," she replied, her voice quieter than usual. "They both passed away several years back. First my mother, then my father shortly after. They had me later in life, so they were already quite a bit older."

Damian felt the weight of her words. "Sorry to hear that."

Her face clouded over, a brief flicker of pain in her eyes. "Thanks."

She pushed open the weathered wooden gate, and they stepped onto the grounds. The house sprawled out before them, once a charming farmhouse but now showing signs of neglect.

"La Loma Viva used to be an old coffee plantation," Thorn explained, her voice tinged with nostalgia. "We did some work on the house after my parents died, but I haven't been back for a while."

He could tell. The front of the property still bore the marks of the renovation—two wide sliding doors that opened onto a cobblestone terrace, offering a breathtaking view of the hills and the sea glittering in the distance. But the upkeep had slipped; weeds poked through the paving stones, and the paint on the doors had started to peel. It was clear that the house had once been cared for, but then left to fend for itself.

"We?" Damian asked, raising an eyebrow.

"Me and my late husband."

CHAPTER 21

Thorn stood in the middle of the living room, letting her eyes take in everything around her. The house was filled with memories—things she and Jaden had picked out together, things they'd used during their stays here. His presence was so strong, it was almost like he was right there with her.

She shivered, despite the warmth of the day. Coming back here was always going to be tough, but she hadn't expected the emotional hit to be this hard.

She could still see him, clear as day—sitting on the couch with a cold beer, tinkering with the boiler when the hot water wouldn't work, laying those paving stones on the terrace outside.

Tears welled up in her eyes, but she only let them fall because she could hear the water running. Damian had gone straight to the bathroom to take a cold shower. There would be no hot water after this long.

Thorn sniffed and took a shaky breath. Maybe if she went outside into the sun, she'd cast off the shadows.

Out on the terrace, the sun hit her full in the face. Blinking, she sat down on the low stone wall and looked out over the terraced fields below—once full of olive trees, now just dried-up remnants of what used to be. She let her feet dangle, staring at the horizon. The view was the same, the house was the same, but everything felt different. Jaden was gone, and she was here with someone else.

The sun dried her tears, but she stayed put until she heard Damian step outside. "You okay?"

"Yeah, I'm just tired. How about we take a nap before we figure out our next move?"

He looked at her for a moment, then nodded. "Yeah, sure. Which room do you want me to take?"

She shot him a surprised look. After last night—she pushed the thought away, not ready to deal with that. She'd assumed he'd want to be with her.

"I think we could both use some alone time." He kept his tone light. "And honestly, I'm just going to crash. I assume we're safe here?"

She gave him a grateful smile. She needed time alone with her thoughts and the memories that haunted this place.

"Yeah, they won't find us here. Not even Pat and the unit know about this spot, and it's in my parents' name, not mine." If anyone was tracking them, they wouldn't get past Las Piedras.

"Okay, then. I'll see you later." And he strode back into the house without another word.

Thorn showered and changed into fresh clothes that she found in the closet, then collapsed onto the bed. The door to the spare room was closed—Damian would be out cold by now.

Why had she brought him here?

Because there was nowhere else to go, she reminded

herself. Damian needed protection, and this was the only place that came to mind where they'd be completely safe. But even knowing she'd done the right thing to protect her high-value target didn't stop her emotions from spiraling.

Despite the years, the bed still carried a faint trace of Jaden's scent. His things were still on the dresser—his comb, his deodorant. She picked up the deodorant before lying down, breathing in the familiar smell, and once again was overwhelmed with sadness.

The bedside table had a stack of books Jaden had planned to read but never got the chance. She ran her fingers over them gently. Like her, he'd loved to read.

It was stiflingly hot in the bedroom, even with the window open, so she reached up and pulled the cord for the ceiling fan. It creaked to life, slowly at first, like it had forgotten how to work, but then picked up speed, sending a light breeze over her.

That was better. She closed her eyes, letting the sound of the fan and the memories swirling around her lull her into a restless sleep.

When Thorn opened her eyes hours later, she thought she was back at the hotel with Damian. Then reality came crashing back, and the warmth of that thought was replaced by the cold, familiar grip of grief.

Pushing it aside, she got up and went outside. Damian was sitting on the terrace. He had set up the outdoor table and chairs, which he must have found stacked in the outdoor shed, and was sitting with a beer in hand.

He smiled when he saw her. For once, her heart didn't do a flip-flop. "It's warm, but right now it's the best damn beer I've ever tasted."

She joined him at the table. "I see you found the outdoor furniture."

"Yeah, I hope you don't mind. It's such a gorgeous evening, and this view." He whistled softly. "It's incredible."

She looked out over the hilly landscape to where the sky met the sea. "It sure is. It's why my parents bought the place. They loved it here."

"I can see why."

Thorn forced her mind back to the practicalities. "We'll need some food. There used to be a local farm store down the road. It should have everything we need."

Damian nodded, his eyes bright and more alert since his nap. He'd cleaned up, too, the stubble gone, probably using one of Jaden's old razors, but he was still wearing the same filthy jeans and shirt.

"You can borrow some of Jaden's clothes," she said, her voice tight. "You can't keep wearing those."

"You sure?"

"It's practical. Besides, it's not like he needs them anymore." She bit her lip, hoping the pain would stop the rising wave of emotion.

Damian put down his beer. "You miss him, don't you? Being back here can't be easy."

She shook her head. He had no idea.

One thing was for sure, she wasn't ready to talk about it, least of all to the man she'd just slept with. "I think I'll head to the store before it shuts."

She felt his eyes on her as she walked back inside to get the motorcycle keys.

Thorn returned with two heavy bags of groceries. She'd just made it to the farm store before closing and had ridden the mile and a half back with one bag hooked over each handlebar.

"Damian?"

The sliding doors were wide open, and she could hear

music playing—one of Jaden's old CDs—but Damian was nowhere in sight.

"In the kitchen," he called back.

She stepped into the kitchen, only to freeze in her tracks. The bags slipped from her hands, groceries spilling across the floor. Standing at the sink was Jaden. No, not Jaden—Damian, but dressed in Jaden's beige cargo shorts and his favorite dusky-blue T-shirt. From the back, it was like seeing a ghost.

"Are you okay?" Damian spun around.

She tried to shake off the shock. "Oh, God. Yes. I'm sorry. You gave me a fright, that's all. Seeing you in those clothes, I thought…" She trailed off, feeling foolish. "It's stupid. I'm fine."

Damian bent down to pick up the groceries. "You thought I was Jaden?"

She nodded, her throat tight.

He stood and placed the bags on the counter, his expression softening. "I'm sorry. I didn't mean to startle you. You said it would be okay."

"It is." She felt like an idiot. Of course, it wasn't Jaden. He was gone. She shook her head to clear it. "I think I'll have that beer now."

Damian opened the fridge and handed her a cold one. "I plugged it in, and it's working. Nice to have electricity out here."

"Yeah, that was a recent thing. They installed it after we did the renovations. Before that, we used generators."

"Why don't you go outside and relax? I'll make us something to eat."

"You cook too?"

He masked a grin. "I know my way around a kitchen. Confirmed bachelor, remember?"

"I can help," she offered, but Damian shook his head.

"You went to get the groceries. I'll do this."

Thorn went outside, secretly relieved. Standing beside him, looking like that—it was too much.

A short time later, he emerged onto the terrace carrying a platter filled with warm tortillas, a bowl of guacamole, and some fresh jicama sprinkled with chili powder and lime. He'd even opened a bottle of tequila he found in the cupboard.

"This looks amazing," Thorn said, eyeing the bottle of tequila. The label read Reserva 2015. The year Jaden died. "I forgot we had this."

Damian grinned. "I figured we could use a little indulgence."

The food was welcome, especially after going so long without anything hearty. When they finished, Damian poured them each another shot and turned to her, his expression suddenly serious.

"I know we need to talk."

"Not now," she whispered. She couldn't face questions about their relationship. "Let's just enjoy the view and the tequila."

He nodded, lifting his glass. "To the view, then. And to forgetting everything else for a while."

They clinked glasses, the smooth burn of the tequila starting to warm her from the inside out. As the evening wore on, they continued to drink, the tension between them loosening with each shot. The stars above seemed to blur together, the crisp night air mixing with the warmth of the alcohol, creating a heady mix that left them both slightly unsteady.

Damian's laughter came easier, his voice softer, and Thorn found herself relaxing into the moment, her guard slipping just a little. The tequila worked its magic, dulling the sharp edges of her grief, making it easier to push the memories of Jaden to the back of her mind. But as Damian poured yet another shot, she knew she couldn't keep avoiding it forever.

He handed her the glass, his fingers brushing hers, and the simple contact sent a shiver through her. She downed the shot, the burn no longer as intense as before, and set the glass down with a sigh.

"Jaden," she started, her voice barely above a whisper. "He... he would have loved this."

Damian turned to her, the playful glint in his eyes replaced by something deeper, more understanding. He didn't interrupt, just waited, letting her find the words.

Thorn took a deep breath, the tequila making her bold, or maybe just tired of holding it all in. "We used to sit out here, just like this. Drinking, laughing... dreaming about the future." Her voice wavered, the weight of the memories pressing down on her. "But that future never came. He was taken too soon."

Damian reached out, his hand covering hers. "I'm sorry," he said softly, his touch grounding her as she fought back tears.

She nodded, swallowing hard. "I don't talk about him much. It's easier to pretend I'm okay, that I've moved on. But the truth is, I'm still stuck in that moment. The year he died... everything changed."

They sat in silence for a moment, the tequila giving her just enough courage to continue. "I don't know how to let him go," she admitted, her voice trembling. "I don't know if I want to."

Damian squeezed her hand, his voice gentle. "You don't have to let him go, Thorn. You just have to find a way to keep living."

She looked at him, her eyes glassy from the drink and the emotions bubbling to the surface. For the first time in a long time, she felt like she wasn't alone in her grief, like someone understood the pain she carried.

With a strangled sob, she buried her face in his shoulder and cried. To her embarrassment, the tears wouldn't stop. She clung to Damian, letting out all the pain she'd held back for so long. He didn't say a word, just held her tight, offering silent comfort as she cried.

CHAPTER 22

*D*amian finally got it.

The reluctance to talk about her past, the stony silences, the wall she'd built around herself—it all made sense now. She'd been through hell, and even five years later, she hadn't fully come to terms with it. Knowing her, he figured she hadn't talked to anyone about it—not a therapist, not her old CIA colleagues, no one. She'd just bottled it up and kept pushing forward, like she always did.

Eventually, she pulled away, wiping her eyes. "I'm sorry." Her voice was shaky. "I'm not usually such a mess. Being here... it's brought everything back. That's why I never returned."

"I get it," Damian said softly.

She gulped, nodding. "I didn't realize how hard it would be. I thought I could handle it. I mean, it's been five years." She shook her head, glancing up at him with a tired expression. "And look at me."

"I don't think we ever truly get over losing someone we love," he said quietly.

She gave a small, sad laugh, somewhere between a chuckle and a sniffle. "Then I'm screwed."

So am I.

Damian felt the weight of his realization.

Out loud, he said, "Jaden was a hero. He died protecting you, the woman he loved."

Her eyes glistened with fresh tears. "I know," she whispered. "I think about that all the time. If I had to go, that's the way I'd want it too."

It was a heroic death, one Damian knew he could never live up to—not that he'd want to. Jaden would always be a hero in her eyes, a man who'd given everything to protect her. And that was where Damian's admiration clashed with something darker. How could he possibly resent a man who'd sacrificed so much?

Yet, as much as he respected Jaden for what he'd done, he also hated him for holding onto Thorn's heart so tightly, even from beyond the grave. How could he be jealous of a dead man? But there it was, gnawing at him, a bitterness he couldn't shake.

She bit her lip, her voice shaky. "I also wonder if, you know, if I hadn't gotten out of the water, maybe Jaden would still be alive."

"You can't think like that, Thorn. What happened wasn't your fault."

"I know." Her voice wavered. "It doesn't stop me from wondering."

He couldn't blame her for replaying that day, wondering how things might've turned out differently. Hadn't he done the same thing a thousand times after Rebecca left?

"Was Jaden a CIA agent too?" He was curious about the man who'd left such a huge void in her life.

She shook her head, a small, wistful smile forming. "No, he was an architect. He worked for a firm that designed these incredible buildings all over the world. We met in Paris. I was on assignment, pretending to be an art dealer, and he was there for a design conference."

"Was it love at first sight?" He wasn't sure why he asked, but the words slipped out.

"Actually, no." She managed a thin smile. "I thought he was a little full of himself—typical creative. But that was before I really knew him."

Hadn't she thought Damian cocky once too?

Damian returned to his chair. Thorn had pulled herself together. Her eyes were red, and she looked pale, but she wasn't on the verge of tears anymore. "Appearances can be deceiving," he said quietly.

"That's true." She sat down too, immediately refilling her glass. "Look, I'm sorry for falling apart like that, especially on assignment. It's embarrassing."

"Don't be, and there's no need to apologize. I'm not just some high-value target you're protecting. I care about you." And he really meant it. Even though they'd only known each other for a few days, they'd been through so much that it felt like months.

She was one of the bravest, smartest, and most beautiful women he'd ever met, and he was falling for her hard.

But it was clear now—there was no room for him in her heart. Not with Jaden still there, an unshakable presence in her life.

How could he compete with a memory?

A surge of jealousy hit, but he drowned it out with another shot of tequila.

"Thanks, Damian." Her voice softened. "That means a lot."

There was a pause, then she spoke again. "Actually, do you mind if I turn in for the night? I'm exhausted."

"Sure, no problem." He didn't even bother asking if she wanted him to join her. He already knew the answer. It was hard enough being in Jaden's house, surrounded by Jaden's things, drinking Jaden's tequila. The last thing she'd want was to complicate things further by having him in the bed she'd shared with her husband. "I'll see you tomorrow."

She gave him a sad smile, got up, and went inside. "See you tomorrow," she said softly before disappearing into the house.

Damian stayed on the terrace, long into the night. By the time he turned in, the tequila bottle was almost empty.

CHAPTER 23

Thorn had drunk several cups of coffee, eaten breakfast, and taken a good look around the property by the time Damian appeared the next morning.

Jeez, he looked rough as hell. She'd found the empty bottle of tequila on the outside table this morning, and guiltily, suspected she might be the cause.

"How's the head?" she asked, glancing up as he came into the living room. She'd been curled up on the couch reading a novel, something she hadn't done in years.

He grimaced in reply.

Wordlessly, she got up, went to the kitchen, and poured him a cup of coffee. He accepted it gratefully and then sank down gingerly on the couch.

"Damian," she began. "I feel bad about last night. I shouldn't have dumped on you like that. I mean, I'm supposed to be protecting you, and—"

"You are protecting me," he said, then winced as if the words were too loud. He lowered his voice. "You got me out of Las Piedras and brought me here. We're safe. I'll probably make it until Friday, so the FBI will be happy."

She frowned at his tone. "Is something wrong?"

"Apart from the elephants parading around in my head, no."

She studied him for a moment. He was pissed about last night, she could tell. She might not be as good at reading him as he was at reading her, but she knew when a man was sulking.

It was Jaden. Why did she have to have a meltdown like that right in front of him? Ever since they'd met, she'd been an emotional wreck. It was pathetic, and oddly, not like her at all.

"You speak to Pat?" he asked, changing the subject before she could dwell on it anymore.

"Yeah, this morning. I told him what had happened, and he was understandably concerned. He's going to look into the possibility of a leak at the office, although I can't think who it could be."

"I wouldn't put it past Alek to try to buy off one of your operatives," he grumbled.

She pursed her lips. "I don't know. Pat vets them pretty thoroughly before he hires them. I doubt any of them can be bought."

He shrugged. "Everyone has a price."

Her eyes slanted. "Not everyone."

He didn't respond. An uneasy silence stretched between them, until Damian said, "I thought I'd clean up the Yamaha today."

"Are you sure?" If he wanted to wash a filthy motorcycle, that was up to him. "We're just going to ditch it anyway."

"The owners will want it back, and I've got nothing better to do."

Another jab, even if it wasn't intentional.

"Okay, fine. I'll be inside if you need me. I've got a lot of sorting to do."

"I won't. We're good here."

She gave a weary nod. "Yeah, we're good."

Thorn watched Damian leave the room, his broad shoulders tense, the unspoken words between them hanging like a heavy fog. She let out a slow breath, her eyes trailing to the door as it clicked shut behind him.

A part of her wanted to call him back, to explain herself, to make him understand that last night had nothing to do with him.

But she couldn't.

Not yet.

The old farmhouse was eerily quiet once Damian was gone. Thorn stood in the center of the living room, feeling the weight of the past pressing in on her from all sides. It wasn't just the house, it was everything that came with it. Every corner, every piece of furniture, every photograph on the wall was a reminder of a life she no longer lived, with a man who no longer existed.

She wasn't sure how long she stood there, lost in thought, before her gaze finally settled on the doorway to the study. The door was slightly ajar, a thin sliver of darkness spilling into the hall. It was the only room she hadn't been able to bring herself to enter since they'd arrived. The study had been Jaden's space, where he'd drafted designs, drawn sketches and sometimes painted. Now, it was just a room full of ghosts.

Thorn crossed the living room, her steps slow and deliberate as she approached the study. She pushed the door open fully, the old hinges creaking. The room was just as she remembered it, though dustier now.

Jaden's desk sat in the corner, drawings still scattered across the surface as if he'd just stepped out for a moment and would return any second to finish his work. The bookshelf along the far wall was filled with his favorite books, spines worn from use. A jacket still hung on the back of the chair.

Her breath caught in her throat as she stepped inside, the familiar scent of leather and draft paper filling her nostrils. For a moment, she stood frozen in the doorway, her fingers clutching the frame as memories came rushing back—Jaden sitting at that desk, lost in thought, the way he'd look up and smile when she walked in, the sound of his voice as he explained the intricacies of one of his sketches.

Move.

Thorn walked over to the desk, her hand hovering over the surface before she finally allowed her fingers to brush against the papers. They were brittle now, the edges yellowed with age.

She picked up a photograph, her chest tightening as she looked at the image of Jaden, smiling at the camera, his arm around her waist. They'd been so happy back then, so sure of their future.

A tear slipped down her cheek, and Thorn quickly brushed it away, but more followed. She clutched the photo to her chest, her breath hitching as the grief she was barely keeping at bay broke through again.

She cried for Jaden, for the life they'd planned together that had been so cruelly taken from them. She cried for the love they'd shared, a love that had been perfect and flawed and everything in between. And she cried for herself, for the woman she'd been before his death, and the woman she was now.

When the tears finally subsided, she was left feeling hollow, exhausted.

She looked down at the photograph, and carefully set it

back on the desk. Slowly, she stood, her legs unsteady as she wiped away the last of her tears.

Enough now.

She knew what she had to do.

It was time.

Thorn found some boxes in the closet and began the task of packing away Jaden's belongings. She started with the books, carefully placing each one into a box. Each title brought back a memory, and she allowed herself to linger on them for a moment before moving on. She packed away his drawings next, trying not to read the notes scribbled in the margins. It was too painful to think about the things he'd never get to finish.

Finally, she reached for the jacket. She hesitated, fingers brushing against the worn leather. Thorn closed her eyes, bringing the jacket to her nose, inhaling deeply. The scent was faint, but it was still there, a reminder of him.

With a deep breath, she folded the jacket and placed it gently on top of the other items in the box.

Next, she moved on to the bedroom and did the same thing there.

Finally, when she was done, she sealed the boxes with tape and stacked them neatly in the study. That room was empty now, stripped of everything that had made it Jaden's.

Now, instead of feeling the crushing weight of loss, she felt lighter, as if a burden had been lifted.

Packing away Jaden's things didn't mean she was forgetting him. She could never do that. But it was a step—a necessary step—toward healing, toward allowing herself to move forward. Toward allowing herself to live again, maybe even love again.

She was ready to let go, not of Jaden, but of the hold the past had on her. And as she left the study, closing the door behind her, she felt a sense of peace she hadn't felt in years.

Back in the living room, Thorn paused, glancing out the window. Damian was still outside, working on the Yamaha. She could see the tension in his shoulders, the way he scrubbed the bike with more force than necessary, as if he could wash away the frustration he felt. She knew she owed him an apology, a real one this time.

But that could wait. For now, she needed a moment to herself, to absorb the enormity of what she'd just done. She sank back onto the couch, her eyes closing as she took a deep breath, feeling the weight of the past finally begin to lift.

Now, at least, she could concentrate on the future.

CHAPTER 24

*D*amian wiped the sweat from his brow with the back of his hand, the damp cloth he'd been using to clean the Yamaha now draped over his shoulder. The sun hung high in the sky, beating down on him with relentless intensity. At least his hangover had started to lift.

He drained the last of his bottle of water, admiring his handiwork.

The bike gleamed, its once-filthy chrome now catching the light in a way that was almost satisfying. He ought to be pleased with his accomplishment, but he couldn't shake the unease that had been gnawing at him all morning.

That's why he'd thrown himself into the task with a determination bordering on obsession, trying to scrub away the remnants of last night's tension.

It hadn't worked.

Coming here... The pain it had unleashed had erected a wall between them, and he was on the outside, unable to scale it.

Anger simmered deep in his gut, but there was nothing he could do about it. He had no right to be jealous of a ghost, yet that didn't stop the sour taste in his mouth every time he thought of Jaden.

Fuck.

His hand tightened around the cloth. It wasn't like him to get so worked up over something—or someone—he couldn't control. But Thorn wasn't just anyone. She had gotten under his skin, burrowed into a place he hadn't thought was still vulnerable. And now, with that unspoken weight hanging between them, he wasn't sure what to do with the feelings she stirred in him.

He glanced up when he heard the soft hiss of the patio door sliding open. Thorn stepped onto the porch, a tall glass of lemonade in each hand, the ice clinking softly as she made her way down the steps.

He tried not to notice the way the sunlight caught in her hair, turning it into a bronze halo around her face.

"Thirsty?" she asked, coming up to him.

"Yeah, thanks." He took the glass and raised it to his lips. The lemonade was cold and tangy, the perfect antidote to the sweltering heat. Downing it in one go, he set the glass down on the ground.

She nodded to the motorcycle. "You've done a great job. It looks brand new."

Damian shrugged. "Needed something to keep me busy."

Thorn's fingers tightened briefly around her glass, but the smile that followed was genuine, if a little bittersweet. "I suppose I'm to blame for that."

"I don't blame you for anything," he said quietly. "It is what it is."

She looked off into the distance, and instead of the pinched expression she'd had since she got here, there was an almost peacefulness about her now.

"I know, but I still owe you an apology." She paused. "I've

done some thinking, and some tidying up, and I'm feeling much better."

He stared, puzzled. "I'm glad."

She gave a self-deprecating chuckle. "No more emotional outbursts, I promise."

"I was glad to be able to help." He paused. "At least, I hope I helped."

A soft smile that made his heart sing. "You did."

Something had shifted between them—he could feel it, even if he didn't fully understand it. For the first time since they'd come to this farmhouse, he allowed himself to hope. Hope that whatever demons she'd conquered would leave a little space in her heart for him.

"How about a run?"

Damian glanced up from the book he'd started reading, one of Jaden's, and broke into a grin. "Sounds good."

The sun was dipping low in the sky when they set off, casting long shadows across the dry, cracked earth. The air was still thick with heat, but it had lost its punishing edge, making it just bearable enough to work out.

Damian fell into an easy rhythm beside Thorn, his boots crunching against the gravel as they made their way down the dusty path leading away from the farmhouse.

It felt great. Damn, did he need this.

The steady thud of his feet on the ground, the way his breath synchronized with Thorn's—there was something oddly calming about it. A little too calming, given the storm of emotions swirling inside him.

He glanced over at Thorn, noting the ease in her stride, the way she seemed almost... light. Maybe she really had moved on. Her shoulders were less rigid, and there was a faint smile that tugged at her lips.

He didn't know what to make of that.

It was like she'd finally let go of whatever had been

holding her back. It made her even more irresistible, and that scared the hell out of him.

"Race you to that old tree?" Her voice cut through his thoughts, light and teasing.

Damian blinked, caught off guard by the challenge. "You serious?"

Her grin widened, and she took off without another word, sprinting ahead of him. For a second, he just stood there, watching her go, the sway of her hips almost hypnotic.

Then his competitive streak kicked in, and he surged forward, his longer strides quickly closing the distance between them.

She was fast, but he had the advantage of power. Within moments, he was right behind her, close enough to hear her laugh—an honest-to-God laugh—something that made his chest tighten in ways he didn't want to examine too closely.

He pushed himself harder, and just as they reached the old, gnarled tree that marked the end of their makeshift race, he caught up to her. They both skidded to a stop, panting and out of breath, grinning like idiots.

Damian couldn't remember the last time he'd felt this free.

"You almost had me there," he said between breaths, leaning forward with his hands on his knees.

Thorn brushed a strand of hair away from her face, her eyes sparkling with something that made his stomach flip. "Almost? I think I did."

"Not quite," he shot back, a playful edge in his tone. "You were just lucky I let you get a head start."

"Is that so?" She raised an eyebrow, still catching her breath. "Well, next time, I won't go so easy on you."

Damian chuckled, shaking his head as he straightened up. His pulse was still racing, but not just from the run. The air buzzed around them, like it had after the live music at the taverna.

He wasn't sure how to handle it, this new side to Thorn—the side that flirted, that smiled like she didn't have the weight of the world on her shoulders.

His body did, however.

Every instinct screamed at him to close the distance between them, to act on the magnetic pull he felt whenever she was near.

But what then? What would that mean? He didn't want to mess this up, didn't want to spoil it by moving too soon.

Still, the tension between them was undeniable, and it was getting harder to ignore. His eyes traced the curve of her neck, the way her skin glistened with sweat in the dimming light. It would be so easy to reach out, to pull her close and find out if the fire between them was still there.

But he didn't. Not yet.

They jogged back in comfortable silence, the night settling around them. When they reached the farmhouse, they were both drenched in sweat, but in an upbeat mood.

"You shower first," he said to her. The old farmhouse only had one bathroom.

"You sure?"

"Yeah, go for it."

Thorn paused at the bathroom door, turning to face him. Her eyes were dancing. "I really enjoyed that."

"Me too."

There was a brief pause, and then she smiled and went inside.

Damian walked into the living room and opened the patio doors wide to let in the cooler air. As he stood there, staring out at the horizon, he knew one thing for sure.

He wasn't out of the game yet.

Not by a long shot.

The air continued to buzz all the way through supper, which they ate on the patio again, washed down with a bottle of wine. And afterward, they sat outside talking softly.

"You never told me why your wife left you," she said when they were halfway through their second glass.

He hesitated. "I don't actually know."

Thorn frowned. "Really?"

"Yeah. She said she was going back to the hotel for a massage. I was scuba diving at the time, I think." He scoffed bitterly at his own naivety. "When I got back to our hotel room, she was gone."

"Weren't you worried?" Thorn looked across at him.

"Not really. She'd packed her things up and left. A taxi had come to collect her. I checked with the hotel concierge."

"Oh."

He ground his jaw. "Yeah."

Her voice dropped to a whisper. "So you have no idea why she left?"

"I think she got cold feet. Maybe she didn't want to be married to me. Who knows? Her father coerced her into it. I know that much."

"Alek made her marry you?" Thorn's eyebrows rose in surprise.

"In a sense. I mean, he sent her to seduce me, and by marrying me, they'd keep me in the family business. I'd have no choice but continue to do Alek's bidding."

"It's so manipulative," she hissed. "What a bastard, using his own daughter like that."

"Yep." Damian nodded. "That pretty much sums him up."

She shook her head. "Did you ever look for her?"

"I did. I got a private investigator to find her a couple of years later. By then I'd already fallen out with Alek."

"You saw her?"

He shook his head. "I got the P.I. to deliver the divorce

papers. Rebecca was flitting around the world, traveling and having fun. She had no issue with signing them."

"Wow," Thorn breathed. "I'm sorry, Damian. That's tough."

"I'm not." He looked over at her, her hair lifting softly in the breeze. There was no denying it, he was falling face-first, head over heels for his beautiful Rose.

His.

When had he started thinking of her as his?

Since that first kiss. Maybe earlier, since their fake marriage. That's why he'd been so uptight about Jaden, because he'd gotten used to having the dead man's wife all to himself, and now he was having to share her again.

Except, maybe not.

Something had shifted in her. He'd known it from the run. He'd never allowed himself to hope so much for something in his life.

Now he needed to know.

But he still didn't want to push it. Didn't want to send her flying back to that dark place she'd been in when they'd arrived at the farmhouse. He needed her to be okay with it.

With him.

So he waited and did nothing.

CHAPTER 25

There was a soft creak as Thorn got out of her chair. The way Damian was looking at her—with heat, etched with worry and a little bit of apprehension—it softened him. It made the growly beast less intimidating, more human.

She wanted to wipe the worry from his eyes, reassure him that she was still there. That she still had feelings for him. That it did mean something.

Coming here had knocked her off course, and for a moment, she feared she'd made a humongous mistake. That her feelings for Damian were nothing more than a fling, a distraction. Something to be fought and squashed and ignored.

But she'd been wrong.

Even with her thoughts full of Jaden, she hadn't been able to stop thinking about Damian. It all made sense now. That's why it had hurt so badly. She hadn't just lost her husband; she'd moved on. That's why she'd been an emotional wreck—because she knew she was letting go. She couldn't hold on to the memories any longer. It was time to make new ones.

That's what hurt the most.

One thing she knew for sure was that Jaden would have wanted her to be happy. He'd tried to make her happy, and he had, for that short time. Now it was someone else's turn.

Thorn's heartbeat quickened as she closed the distance between them. Damian's eyes darkened, his jaw tightening as if he was bracing for something. Maybe he thought she was going to walk away again, leave him hanging like she had before. But that wasn't going to happen—not this time.

She didn't break eye contact, her breath catching as she took in the rugged lines of his face, the tension coiled in his broad shoulders. There was something raw about him, something that always made her pulse race. It was like looking at a storm about to break, and for once, she wanted to be right in the middle of it.

Without a word, she slid onto his lap, her thighs pressing against his hips as she straddled him. She felt the sharp intake of his breath, saw the flicker of surprise in his eyes before they darkened further, the heat between them sparking to life.

Her hands found their way to his shoulders, fingers curling into the fabric of his shirt as she leaned in, her lips hovering just above his.

For a split second, she hesitated. Maybe this was crazy, maybe she was moving too fast, but the way he was looking at her, with that mix of desire and caution, told her he wanted her as much as she wanted him.

She didn't need words to show him what she felt—words had never been their strong suit anyway.

So she kissed him.

It wasn't soft or tentative. This was all fire and need, the turmoil of the last two days erupting inside her. She poured everything into that kiss—every fear, every doubt, every longing she'd tried to suppress.

Damian's response was immediate, his hands gripping her hips, pulling her closer until there was no space left between them. She felt his fingers digging into her butt, anchoring her against his hard, erect cock.

She gasped, her mind going blank. Her world narrowed down to the feel of his mouth on hers, the way his stubble scraped against her skin, grounding her in the moment.

She kissed him harder, deeper, wanting to erase any doubts he might still have. This wasn't just about making a point—this was her way of telling him that she was here, that she wanted him, that she wasn't going anywhere.

She needn't have worried. Damian got the message, loud and clear.

Her mind raced, thoughts colliding in a blur of emotions. This was real—more real than anything she'd felt in a long time. The fear of moving on, of betraying Jaden's memory, had kept her locked in a cage of grief for too long. But now, here with Damian, she realized that moving forward didn't mean forgetting. It meant living, feeling, and allowing herself to love again. The realization was both terrifying and exhilarating.

What if this was just another mistake? What if she was wrong? But deep down, she knew she wasn't.

Not this time.

Thorn didn't give him time to think—didn't give herself time to second-guess. She reached for the hem of her shirt and pulled it over her head, tossing it aside without a second thought. Damian's eyes darkened, his breath catching as he took in the sight of her, his hands instinctively tightening on her hips.

She slid her fingers under the collar of his shirt, tugging it off him in one swift motion. Their breaths mingled as she leaned in, pressing her bare chest against his, the heat of their skin searing together. Damian's hands roamed up her back, rough palms skimming over her curves as she straddled him, her thighs tightening around his waist.

The chair creaked under their combined weight, but neither of them cared. Thorn could feel the tension coiling in her stomach, an electric charge that surged through her veins as she ground her hips against him. The thin fabric of his jeans did little to mask the hardness beneath, and she reveled in the way he responded to her, a low growl rumbling deep in his chest.

Damian's hands moved to the waistband of her pants, his fingers deftly undoing the button and sliding the zipper down. Thorn lifted her hips just enough for him to slide them off, leaving her in nothing but her underwear. His gaze was hungry, almost predatory, as he took her in—every inch of her exposed skin, every curve and dip of her body.

She could feel the air between them thicken, the tension growing unbearable. Thorn reached down, her fingers trailing over the front of his jeans, feeling the hard outline of him beneath the denim. She undid his belt, her movements slow and deliberate, savoring the way his breath hitched with every touch.

When she finally freed him from the confines of his jeans, Damian let out a groan that was half relief, half anticipation. Thorn didn't waste any time—she positioned herself over him, her body trembling with anticipation as she guided him to her entrance.

For a moment, they just hovered there, on the edge of something explosive. Thorn locked eyes with him, her breath catching as she slowly lowered herself onto him, taking him inch by inch. The sensation was overwhelming, a heady mix of pleasure and pain as her body stretched to accommodate him. Damian's hands gripped her hips, his fingers digging into her skin as he fought to keep control.

Thorn began to move, her pace slow and deliberate,

teasing him with every roll of her hips. The friction was exquisite, every movement sending sparks of pleasure shooting through her. Damian's breathing grew ragged, his control slipping as he thrust up to meet her, matching her rhythm with a desperate intensity.

She leaned in, capturing his mouth in a fierce kiss, their tongues tangling as they moved together in a raw, primal dance. The chair creaked beneath them, the sound mixing with their heavy breathing, their groans of pleasure filling the room. Thorn could feel the tension building in her core, a tight coil of heat that threatened to snap at any moment.

Damian's hands roamed up her back, one sliding into her hair to pull her closer, deepening the kiss. The other moved to her breast, his thumb brushing over her nipple in a way that made her gasp against his mouth. He swallowed the sound, his own groan vibrating against her lips as he thrust deeper, harder, driving her closer to the edge.

Thorn's movements grew frantic, her hips grinding against him as she chased the release that was just out of reach. The pleasure was almost too much, too intense, but she didn't want it to end. She wanted to stay in this moment forever, lost in the heat of Damian's touch, the feel of him inside her, the connection that went beyond anything she'd ever felt before.

When the climax finally hit, it was like a wave crashing over her, pulling her under. Thorn threw her head back, a cry tearing from her throat as the pleasure consumed her, leaving her trembling and breathless in its wake. Damian followed her over the edge, his grip on her tightening as he found his own release, his head falling back against the chair with a guttural groan.

For a moment, they just stayed there, bodies entwined, breathing hard as the aftershocks of their climax rippled through them. Thorn's forehead rested against Damian's, their breaths mingling in the space between them. The tension that had been there earlier was gone, replaced by a deep, unspoken understanding—a bond that went beyond words.

Thorn knew, in that moment, that everything had changed. And for the first time, she was okay with that.

CHAPTER 26

Damian didn't want to leave the farmhouse, and he sensed the same hesitation in Thorn. The last two days had been magical—the best of his life—and he couldn't bear the thought of that ending. The idea of not being able to hold her in his arms, make love to her whenever they felt like it, hear her scream out his name as she exploded beneath him, was almost unbearable.

But there was no choice.

CryptoCon was two days away, and Thorn had just gotten off the burner phone with Pat. "We're to make our way to an abandoned airstrip on the outskirts of the city," she told him, a wry grin on her face. "It was once used by drug dealers, apparently."

He pulled her down onto his lap. "I wish we didn't have to go."

"I know. Me too. But this is your chance to put all this behind you," she said. "To end it once and for all. After this, you'll be free."

Free of the criminal charges. Free from the bad guys chasing him. Free from Alek.

Would Alek stop? That was the question he couldn't answer. It gnawed at him like an angry mosquito bite. Would Alek's desperation to prevent the upgrade turn to anger? Revenge?

Were his days numbered anyway?

He looked at the sparkle in Thorn's eyes, and his chest tightened. What if the same thing happened again? What if he were gunned down in front of her?

He couldn't do that to her again.

Damian exhaled, then gave a stiff nod. "Yeah, that's the plan."

She shot him a quizzical look, then kissed him on the lips. He held her for a fraction longer than necessary, savoring the moment. "It'll be fine. I promise."

It was nearly noon when they set off for the airstrip. They packed the bare minimum, only what they could fit into a small bag that Thorn would carry on her back since he was driving.

The road was bumpy, and she clung to him, her arms wrapped around his waist, as they sped down the dusty road on the Yamaha. The engine roared beneath them, a constant, growling reminder of where they were going and the danger that lay ahead.

Damian narrowed his eyes as the wind whipped past, tugging at their hair and forcing them to lean into each curve of the winding road that cut through the barren landscape.

Thorn's arms tightened around his waist as the road grew rougher, and he tried unsuccessfully to ignore the ache in his chest. Despite the urgency of their journey, part of him wanted to slow down, to stretch out these last few moments together before they were thrust back into the chaos of the world he was trying to escape.

Nothing in his future was certain. For a man who thrived on control, that was maddening. The only thing he was certain of was Thorn's feelings for him. She'd proved it over and over again in the last few days. It was in the way she smiled at him, the way she snuggled into him at night after their lovemaking, still aglow from the last orgasm he'd given her. The way she held his hand when there was no reason to.

Fuck. He'd never had that before.

Never even thought it possible.

He'd closed that side off after Rebecca had left, and somehow the prickly woman he'd been assigned had broken through all that and torn open his soul.

He snorted as he thought about their fake marriage and how far they'd come. The safe room, the drone, the Mexican hotel, and their mad escape over the mountain to the farmhouse—a lifetime of chaos squeezed into one week.

Even now, he could feel her heart beating through his back as they flew down the dusty road.

They passed through a small, dilapidated village—little more than a handful of crumbling buildings and a few stray dogs that didn't bother chasing after them.

The village gave way to open fields, the air growing cooler as the sun dipped below the horizon. The dirt road became more treacherous, riddled with potholes and strewn with debris. It wasn't a problem; he was used to riding and navigated the obstacles with ease.

The landscape around them grew increasingly desolate, the only signs of life the occasional flicker of movement in the brush—a stray coyote or a vulture perched high on a rock. Thorn's grip on him never faltered, which helped to still the dark thoughts that threatened to overwhelm him.

Somehow, he had to survive. He had something to live for now. Someone.

Finally, he could see a future with Thorn, and it was bright. They hadn't talked about it, but they both knew it was a possibility. Something to be explored after the conference. After this madness was over.

He didn't want to lose that.

Hell, he didn't want her to lose that.

Finally, as the last sliver of sun disappeared, they crested a small hill and spotted the airstrip in the distance. It was little more than a cracked strip of asphalt, bordered by rusted chain-link fencing—the remnants of its former life as a smuggler's runway.

A single small plane sat at the far end, its silhouette stark against the darkening sky.

Damian slowed the bike as they approached. This was it.

Once they boarded that plane, their time together was over. For now.

The sound of the Yamaha's engine echoed in the stillness as they rolled to a stop near the plane. Damian cut the engine, the sudden silence jarring after the constant roar of the ride.

Thorn slid off the bike first, her feet hitting the ground with a soft crunch. She stretched, working out the tension from the ride, then turned to face him.

Her eyes met his, and for a moment, they just looked at each other.

"This is it," she whispered, a sad smile tugging at her lips.

He wanted to say something, to reassure her, to promise that everything would be okay, but the words died in his throat.

There were no guarantees.

Instead, he reached out, his hand finding hers and squeezing gently.

"Let's go."

The pilot stepped out of the plane, a grizzled man with a cigarette dangling from his lips. Thorn went up to him, and they spoke for a moment, no doubt checking credentials.

Damian steeled himself. It was time to face the music.

CHAPTER 27

The aircraft touched down at Miami International Airport in the middle of a thunderstorm. Thorn watched the rain lash against the small windows, the turbulence rattling the plane as it taxied down the runway. She shivered.

That better not be a sign of things to come.

As soon as the wheels hit the tarmac, she breathed a sigh of relief. They'd made it. Now they had to face a different kind of tension as they remained on full alert.

Damian leaned back in his seat, his jaw clenched, eyes scanning the storm-drenched landscape outside. For a moment, Thorn felt like they were stepping into a battlefield.

The plane rolled to a stop far from the main terminals, coming to rest near a secluded hangar where a convoy of black SUVs and an armored van awaited.

Blackthorn Security.

Hawk, Pat, and two other men she didn't recognize—all wearing tactical gear with earpieces—approached the plane.

She glanced at Damian, who met her gaze with a slight nod. He was thinking the same thing.

Let's do this.

The sooner they were secure in the conference hotel, the better.

The pilot cut the engine, and the door creaked open, letting in the humid Miami air. Pat and Hawk boarded the plane and motioned for Thorn and Damian to follow.

"Good trip?" Pat asked as she picked up her bag.

She nodded. "Fine."

"Glad to see you safe and sound," Hawk added.

She shot him a brief smile. "Thanks."

There was no time for small talk—they had to get to the sanctuary of the hotel. Thorn followed Damian out into the storm. The rain hit her skin like cold needles, the wind whipping her hair into her face as they hustled down the steps and into the waiting vehicle.

"See you at the hotel," Pat said as he slammed the door shut behind them, sealing them inside the sleek, armored cocoon with blackened windows.

Thorn knew they'd be escorting the van to the hotel, providing backup cover if needed, in case they were ambushed along the route.

The driver took off immediately, the vehicle jerking forward as it merged with the convoy. Thorn could barely make out the city through the rain-streaked windows, the palm trees bending under the force of the storm, the lights of Miami blurred into a kaleidoscope of colors.

Damian sat silently beside her, his gaze fixed on the road ahead. She could see the tension in the set of his shoulders, the way his hands flexed against his knees.

She reached out, her fingers brushing against his.

He glanced at her, his expression softening for just a moment before he turned back to the window. She'd never seen him this on edge before. The easy-going, confident attitude was gone, replaced by a bundle of pent-up, nervous energy.

This meant a lot to him, clearly. She got that.

"We're nearly there," she said, breaking the silence in the back. The driver had the partition down, so he couldn't hear them.

He grunted.

"It'll be okay," she repeated, thinking he was scared, even though it was very unlike him. In all the time she'd known him, he'd never shown any sign of fear.

"That's not what I'm afraid of," he said quietly.

"What then?" She frowned. Was something else bothering him?

"I don't want to be another disappointment."

What was he talking about?

"I want to be there for you, Rose. Do you think that's possible? After all this is over... do you think we can build a life together?"

Her breath caught in her throat. "Damian, now isn't the time—"

"If I make it—"

"You're going to make it. Don't be silly. Twenty-four hours and you'll be in the clear."

He nodded, a distant look in his eyes. The armored vehicle ate up the miles. They were crossing a long causeway over grey-blue water—the color of Damian's eyes—whipped up by the storm.

Her heart soared. He wanted to be with her, wanted to make a life together. That was huge. Even though they'd only known each other for just over a week, they'd been through so much. She knew one should never fall in love during times of crises—it put a false sense of urgency on everything. What they felt now might be enhanced by the situation they were in.

Still, she knew she wanted to be with him, so she didn't care about that. At the very least, they could see where this led. They owed each other that much.

"It's in the corporate website," he whispered, as the wheels drummed over the joins in the road.

Thorn shook her head, not understanding. "What is?"

"The code."

Her heart skipped a beat. "You mean the code for the software update?"

He gave a tight nod. "I hid it in one of the files on the server used to house the website. It's called footer.css. No one ever updates the footer style sheet."

That was clever. Thorn didn't know what a footer style sheet was, but she could guess it was part of the website, probably the bottom section that contained the information about the company. That information never changed and so was never updated. He'd hidden the code in plain sight.

"Remember your promise." His gaze was earnest. "If anything happens to me—"

"Nothing is going to happen to you."

"You don't know that." The look on his face made her wince.

"I do know that. You're going to get to make your announcement. The upgrade will go ahead."

"Promise me, Thorn." His eyes were hard, silver slits.

"I promise," she whispered.

Things happened fast once they got to the hotel. The armored vehicle dipped into an underground parking lot, and flanked by a group of Blackthorn Security operatives, Damian was ushered into the elevator and taken up to the suite.

"Thorn, a word."

It was Pat Burke, her boss.

"Yes, sir." Together, they took the stairs up to the hotel lobby.

"Good work," he said as they walked toward the bar. "Quick thinking in Las Piedras. What the hell happened there?"

She repeated what she'd told him on the phone, going into more detail, describing the two men and the weapons they were carrying. "Damian thinks they could be Alek Markov's men. All I know is they were trained. Definitely hired mercs."

"You'll be pleased to hear the hotel proprietress was unharmed. They searched the hotel and left. Good work stashing your bags in the closet. The local police found them when they searched the room."

"Did they identify us?" she asked, worriedly.

He smiled, but his eyes remained untouched. Pat wasn't known for his warmth. "No, you didn't leave anything telling behind."

She breathed a sigh of relief.

"How's our favorite crypto billionaire holding up?"

She hesitated, but only for a fraction of a second. "He's good. Keeping it together, although I can tell he's worried."

"The FBI are chomping at the bit to get hold of him. They want the upgrade code, in case anything happens to him."

She stiffened, swallowing over the lump in her throat. "Then we'll have to make sure nothing does happen to him."

If she told him she knew where the code was, Damian's life would suddenly become less important. The FBI would swoop in, make a copy, and be less concerned about his welfare than they would be if they thought he was the only one who knew it.

Pat nodded. "That's the goal."

They went over some security details, and he asked her if

she wanted a break. Needed some time off. They could take it from here.

"I'm good," she said firmly. "I'd like to see this through. After all, it would seem strange if his wife suddenly returned home while he was here on his own."

Pat nodded, pleased. "We could definitely use the help, and you know him better than anyone."

She didn't respond.

"How'd you two get on, anyway? Hawk said he thought there was some tension between you back at the house."

"Oh, fine." She tried to disarm him with a smile. "That was just us setting our boundaries. It's always difficult at the start of a new assignment."

He nodded, but she got the feeling he didn't quite believe her.

"So you're good now?"

"Yes, absolutely."

More than good.

An image of Damian's dark head between her legs flashed into her mind, and she clenched her thighs together, praying Pat wouldn't see through her.

Now was not the time to be thinking about that.

"Good." He got up. "I'm sure you'll want to freshen up and get a couple of hours sleep. I've booked you into a room—Anna's got the details."

"Thank you, sir."

"No problem. Come up to the suite first thing tomorrow." He glanced at his watch. "Make that today. We need to discuss strategy for Damian's announcement and the actual upgrade."

"Will do." Her heart lurched at the thought of not spending the night with Damian, but that couldn't be helped. They had to pretend again, but this time, instead of pretending they were together, they had to pretend they were apart.

CHAPTER 28

The day had passed uneventfully. Damian had been confined to his hotel room, his focus split between his laptop and the looming threat of Alek Markov. He'd spent hours meticulously preparing for the upgrade, fine-tuning every detail to ensure it would go off without a hitch.

But even as he worked, a sense of impending danger gnawed at him. Blackthorn Security had been stationed in the adjoining room for most of the day, their low voices murmuring through the walls as they reviewed protocols, planned contingencies, and coordinated with the FBI.

Their presence should have been reassuring, but it only underscored the gravity of the situation. Every time he heard the faint crackle of their radios or the rustle of tactical gear, he felt the tension rise.

He'd caught only brief glimpses of Thorn throughout the day, and each time, it left him feeling more unsettled.

She was focused, professional, her demeanor cool and composed as she coordinated with her team. Annoyingly, they hadn't had a single moment together since they'd arrived.

The sense of impending danger hung over him like a storm cloud, and as night fell, it only grew heavier. Everybody knew that if Alek was going to make a final, last-ditch attempt to get to him, it would be tonight.

Room service had come and gone, but he had no appetite. Even the FBI's visit to brief him on the logistics of their plan—his transfer into custody post-announcement to help them dismantle Alek's network—did little to ease his anxiety.

It was a necessary evil, the price for his freedom and a chance at a future with Thorn, but he wasn't looking forward to it.

Time ticked on. He was still working in the early hours, his mind too restless to sleep, when a loud clanging made him jump.

The fire alarm.

Seconds later, Pat barged into his room, face grim.

"It's him," Damian hissed, rising to his feet. "It has to be."

Pat didn't disagree.

Damian was fully dressed in track pants and a long-sleeved shirt, ready for a quick getaway. He'd anticipated this moment, not that it helped the spiraling tension or the ringing in his ears.

"Anna, sit rep," Pat barked, touching his earpiece, his voice low and clipped. "Copy that." He looked up at Damian. "It's not a drill. There's smoke in the downstairs corridors. We need to evacuate."

Shit.

"Would they really set the place on fire just to get to me?" Damian asked, his voice tinged with disbelief, but he knew the answer. Alek wouldn't hesitate to put countless lives at risk if it meant he could prevent this upgrade from happening.

"They might. Who knows what these fuckers are thinking?" Pat held out an arm, ushering him out of the bedroom and into the adjoining room that had been converted into a tactical command post.

His gaze immediately fell on Thorn. She looked ready for action—hair tied up, wearing tight jeans and a navy T-shirt that showed off her long, lean arms. A holster around her waist carried her Glock, and he could see the earpiece nestled in her ear, connected to the tactical channel.

She flashed him a quick smile before turning back to her team. "My guess is they're going to flush everyone out and take Damian down during the chaos," Hawk was saying, checking the slide on his sidearm.

Damian tensed. Nobody had briefed him on the specifics of the escape plan, so he stood there, helpless, as the team mobilized around him.

"Everyone stick to the plan," Pat barked.

Nods all around.

Wait? There was a plan?

"Put this on." Hawk handed him a Kevlar vest like the ones the team was wearing, along with a red baseball cap bearing a white dolphin logo.

Damian pulled it on, fumbling slightly. "What are we doing? Why the cap?" He glanced at the cap skeptically, wondering how it was supposed to help. If this was a disguise, it was pretty damn weak.

"Just follow our lead," Hawk said, his tone leaving no room for argument.

"Do it," Thorn breathed as she brushed past him.

He knew better than to argue. These guys were pros—he could only hope they knew what they were doing.

Pat cracked open the door, revealing a corridor full of panicked guests rushing toward the stairwell, their footsteps echoing off the walls.

"Keep an eye out for anyone posing as emergency personnel," Hawk warned. "The shooter will probably be dressed as a firefighter or hotel security."

"Got it," Pat replied, his voice booming over the startled murmurs from the guests. "Let's move."

Hawk grabbed Damian's left arm, Thorn took his right, while Pat brought up the rear. They moved cautiously into the corridor, keeping their eyes sharp for anything out of the ordinary.

The faint smell of smoke hung in the air, mingling with the thundering fire alarm and the growing wail of approaching sirens.

Two operatives who had been stationed outside the suite took the lead, sweeping the hallway with their weapons raised. Guests scattered at the sight of the guns, their faces a mix of fear and confusion.

"Stay clear!" Pat ordered, his voice cutting through the mayhem as they pressed forward toward the stairwell.

The smell of smoke grew stronger as they descended. Damian's heart pounded in his chest like a drum, the adrenaline fine-tuning his senses.

The two operatives led the way down the stairwell, their movements practiced and fluid. One of them paused on the landing, checking the area before signaling it was clear.

It was only two floors down to the emergency exit, but with the smoke thickening and visibility diminishing, it felt like miles.

They pushed forward, merging with the crowd of evacuees heading for the exit. Suddenly, a powerful arm grabbed Damian and yanked him sideways into a dark storeroom. At the same moment, one of the other operatives, dressed similarly to Damian in track pants, a black T-shirt, and an identical red cap, seamlessly took his place between Hawk and Thorn.

Damian started to shout, but a hand clamped over his

mouth, and a voice hissed in his ear, "Shut up and stay down."

Realizing this was part of the plan—albeit one he hadn't been briefed on—Damian complied, dropping into a crouch as the storeroom door slammed shut, plunging them into pitch darkness.

Seconds later, gunfire erupted in the corridor outside.

CHAPTER 29

*I*cicles clutched at his heart.

Thorn!

She was out there, in the middle of a barrage of bullets.

He lunged for the door, adrenaline and fear pumping through his veins like ice water, but strong arms yanked him back, slamming him against the wall with a force that knocked the breath out of him.

"Stay down!" a voice barked, leaving him no choice but to comply.

He gritted his teeth, his heart pounding against his ribcage like a jackhammer.

Dear God, please let her be okay.

The sound of rapid gunfire filled the air, punctuated by the shouts of men giving orders and the screams of the unsuspecting. Damian's imagination ran wild—he could see Thorn out there, caught in the crossfire, her body jerking as bullets tore through the air around her.

He had no idea what was happening, and the not knowing was tearing him apart. Every instinct screamed at him to go to her, to fight his way through the chaos and protect her. But the arm across his chest was an iron bar, pinning him in place, forcing him to stay put.

Another burst of gunfire.

Then... silence.

An ominous, deafening silence.

Damian's pulse roared in his ears.

Had they been hit? Were there casualties?

Was Thorn—

A sharp knock on the storeroom door shattered his frantic thoughts. The door creaked open, and Anna stood there, a reassuring smile on her face. "We got them. It's clear. You can come out now."

Damian didn't wait for more. He bolted past her into the smoke-filled corridor, his only thought to find Thorn. The air was thick, choking, and he could barely see through the haze, but then he caught a flash of red hair—a beacon in the chaos.

Thorn was kneeling beside Hawk, who was alive but wincing in pain.

"Bastards," Hawk muttered, his voice rough as he rubbed his chest where the bullet had struck.

Damian skidded to a stop beside them, barely resisting the urge to sweep Thorn into his arms, overwhelmed with relief that she was okay. His pulse was still hammering from the adrenaline. Instead, he placed a shaky hand on her shoulder, needing that physical connection to confirm she was really there, really unharmed.

"What happened?" he demanded, his voice tight, still raw from fear.

Thorn looked up at him, her expression calm but eyes sharp, alert. "They attacked, just like we figured. Hawk took a bullet to the chest, but the vest held. Viper's got a flesh wound, but he'll be fine. We took down two of their guys."

Damian's gaze drifted down the corridor to where two

men in firemen's uniforms lay sprawled on the ground, their bodies riddled with bullet holes—center mass, headshots. Blackthorn Security hadn't taken any chances. The bastards were probably dead before they even hit the floor.

The smoke was getting thicker, making it harder to breathe. Damian coughed, the acrid taste of burning plastic and fabric stinging his lungs.

"Let's get outside." Pat's voice was rough as he pulled a coughing Hawk to his feet.

"Sorry for the deception," Thorn shouted over her shoulder as they sprinted past the real firemen moving into the lobby, hoses at the ready.

Damian didn't get a chance to respond. Water gushed from the hoses just as they reached the exit, the cold spray hitting them like a wall as they pushed through the door—the last ones out of the building.

The night air was a shock to the system, cool and clean compared to the smoke-filled inferno they'd just escaped. Damian took a deep breath, his heart still pounding from everything that had happened.

Thorn was beside him, her hair damp from the spray, but her eyes were bright and determined. He just wanted to take her into his arms and hold her, until the madness had quietened down.

"We knew they'd try to ambush us in the downstairs corridor," she explained. "It was the weak point in our escape route. Instead of avoiding it, we decided to turn it against them."

"It was our chance to take out these bastards," Pat added with a grim grin. Anna was already on her phone, talking to emergency services about retrieving the bodies of the two thugs.

"I recognize them from Las Piedras," Thorn said, her voice tight with anger. "Possibly Markov's men."

"Markov's liquidating his assets as we speak," Pat said, filling them in as he surveyed the scene. "He's getting ready to run. Covering his tracks in case this attempt failed and your update goes live."

"Bastard can't be allowed to get away with it," Damian growled, running a hand through his smoke-scented hair. The fear that had gripped him moments before morphed into something harder, more dangerous.

Rage.

He wasn't just a target anymore, he was a man with a mission, and Markov was in his crosshairs.

"Let's bring the update forward," he snapped. "The conference will have to be postponed, and I want to do it now."

Pat gave him a hard look. "I'm sure that can be arranged. I'll talk to the FBI."

Damian nodded. He was ready to take his scumbag former father-in-law down.

CHAPTER 30

Thorn listened to Damian's announcement, her heart swelling with pride. He stood tall on the stage, his voice steady and confident as he addressed the crowd.

"I know this is a big change, but my team and I believe it's the right move. Lydian will continue to grow, ensuring safe and secure transactions across its global network while also remaining a high-performing investment. The added transparency, similar to what you see with other cryptocurrencies, will help us crack down on illegitimate use that fuels criminal activity and terrorism. As an ethical company, we're committed to this path, and we hope you'll stick with us on this journey. Thank you."

As his words echoed through the conference room, the audience erupted into muted cheers. Thorn could sense the undercurrent of shock. It would take a while for the implications to fully sink in. Right now, Lydian's dark web users were likely in a frenzy, scrambling to sell off their currency, sending its value plummeting. Thorn knew Damian was okay with that. He'd prepared for it. This crash—potentially one of epic proportions—was a necessary evil, a cleansing fire that would burn away the corruption tainting his creation.

She glanced at him from the sidelines, taking in the determined set of his jaw, the way his eyes scanned the crowd, unwavering. He looked every bit the leader he was, standing there behind the bulletproof screen with Hawk and Phoenix—another operative who'd flown in that morning—beside him. *Damn if he didn't look good.* Longing hit her in the gut, a physical ache that made her fingers twitch with the need to touch him. To pull him into her arms and tell him how proud she was. But she had to be patient. Everyone wanted a piece of him right now—Pat, the FBI, his company. And nobody knew about their relationship. They had to keep it under wraps until this whole assignment was well and truly over.

After the fire had been extinguished and the chaos subsided, the hotel had returned to some semblance of normalcy. CryptoCon had resumed, and Damian's announcement had been rescheduled for this morning. The timing was almost poetic—Alek Markov had failed in his assassination attempt, and now, Damian was pushing forward with his vision, undeterred.

The upgrade Damian had installed with James, his brilliant head developer, was already live. Thorn marveled at the complexity of what they had accomplished. The update was designed to insert a transparent ledger into the previously anonymous transactions, stripping away the veil that had allowed criminals to hide in plain sight. It was a masterstroke, a way to weaponize Lydian against those who sought to use it for nefarious purposes. The transition had been seamless, the code slipping into the system without causing a ripple.

Damian had ensured that Lydian would rise from the

ashes, just like the Phoenix statue in his Silicon Valley headquarters.

Thorn's grin widened as she caught Damian's eye from across the room. There was a secret smile there, a knowing look that made her heart sing. But just as she was about to step forward, the FBI agents moved in.

"Mr. Clayton, if you'll come with us."

He didn't resist, and Thorn's heart clenched with the weight of what was coming next. She knew the drill.

The FBI would take him into custody, not as a suspect, but as a critical asset. Damian's help was essential in unmasking Lydian's more infamous users—criminals, terrorists, people who had been hiding behind the cryptocurrency's shield of anonymity for far too long. Alek Markov was now the FBI's Most Wanted, and Damian was their key to bringing him down.

Thorn watched as he was led away, the media descending like vultures, microphones thrust forward, eager for a statement.

"Mr. Clayton, how do you see the changes you've announced today influencing the industry in general?"

"Damian, will Lydian survive this shock announcement?"

The frenzy had begun.

Thorn was grateful that the focus was on the upgrade, on the future of Lydian, rather than the drama that had unfolded only a week ago with their spontaneous wedding. But as much as she wanted to go to him, she held back.

It wasn't their time. Yet.

As he disappeared into the crowd of agents and reporters, Pat tapped her on the shoulder, breaking her out of her thoughts. "Debrief. Let's go."

She nodded, casting one last lingering look at the man she loved before following her boss into the hallway.

She wouldn't get a chance to talk to Damian until after

the FBI were done with him, and that could take days, if not weeks. The Feds were taking him to Washington, D.C., which was fine—Blackthorn Security was based there too, close to the halls of power. But the separation gnawed at her, the uncertainty of when she'd see him again.

The debrief was over quickly, Pat running through the key points with military precision, before dismissing them for some personal time. They were due back at the office in D.C. on Monday, but for now, they had a few hours to themselves.

Thorn headed up to her room to collect her stuff when Hawk sidled up to her, his expression casual but his eyes sharp.

"So, when are you going to see Clayton again?"

She glanced sideways at him, playing it cool. "I don't know what you mean."

"Come on. I saw the way you two were looking at each other. That kiss? The one in the wedding photo? *Phew!*" He fanned himself.

"Oh, that."

"Yeah, that."

"It was nothing," she said, but even to her own ears, it sounded weak, unconvincing.

Hawk smirked. "Don't bullshit a bullshitter, Thorn. I can see what's happening here. You've fallen for him big time, haven't you?"

Her heart skipped a beat. Was she that transparent? The thought sent a ripple of unease through her. She was supposed to be a professional, supposed to keep her emotions in check. "That's bullshit," she replied, but her laugh was uneasy, forced.

"You should go to him."

She sighed, rubbing her temples. There was no point in denying it. Hawk had her pegged.

"I can't, he's in custody." Then, after a beat, "Does Pat know?" Somehow, her boss saw everything. He was like some omniscient being who knew exactly what was going on with all his operatives, even the new ones.

"He suspects, I think, but I haven't said anything."

"Thank you," she breathed, relief flooding through her. "I don't want to get into trouble. This is my first assignment for the agency."

"You won't. My lips are sealed."

She shot him a grateful grin before heading back to her room. But the thought of Damian being in custody, away from her, dragged her down. She was due back at work on Monday, and he'd be tied up with the FBI for the foreseeable future. After that, he'd probably go back to his mansion in San Francisco.

How would they ever find the time to see each other?

The thought weighed on her, but she pushed it aside. At least they didn't have this threat hanging over them anymore. Damian was safe. Or as safe as he could be under the circumstances.

Markov would be on the run, scrambling to cover his tracks. There was no point in sending more thugs after Damian. They just had to bide their time, and then they could be together. Somehow, they'd make it work.

CHAPTER 31

Three weeks later...

THORN'S FLIGHT touched down at San Francisco International Airport just after 8:30 PM. The skies over California were pitch black, the sun long set, and the crisp evening air was a stark contrast to the Miami humidity she'd left behind.

As she stepped off the plane, a knot of anxiety tightened in her chest, making it hard to breathe. She hadn't seen Damian in three weeks. Apart from a few rushed phone calls, they'd barely spoken.

Would it still be the same between them?

Would that magnetic pull still be there, drawing her in like before?

After clearing customs, she caught a cab to Damian's place in the hills. He'd spent the last few weeks in custody at FBI headquarters, helping their analysts dig through the mountain of data they'd pulled from Lydian's servers.

Damian was a key asset in their efforts to unmask Lydian's criminal users, and his knowledge was invaluable. But even knowing that, she couldn't shake the unease gnawing at her insides. What if things had changed while he was away? What if he'd had time to rethink everything—to rethink *them*?

The taxi dropped her off outside the gate of Damian's property. The driveway was dark, no paparazzi in sight. The media frenzy had died down, the news cycle having shifted away from his spontaneous wedding to the bombshell he'd dropped at the conference in Miami. But the security shack was still there, standing guard at the entrance like a silent sentinel, though it was empty now.

She stood for a long moment, trying to figure out her next move.

Should she call him? Or just go to the door?

She'd rehearsed this moment in her head a hundred times, but now that she was here, every plan seemed inadequate.

"This is ridiculous," she huffed, pulling out her phone. "Just call him, for God's sake."

She dialed his number and held her breath.

No answer. After a few rings, it went to voicemail.

That was strange. Wasn't he home? Had she come at a bad time?

She hesitated, then hung up. What she had to say was too important for a message.

Damn.

She felt like a teenager on a first date, sitting there in the dark, unsure of her next move.

She got out of the car and pressed the buzzer on the gate. She heard it ringing in the shack and cursed under her breath. They must have redirected the circuit, so the shack controlled who got in. Damian wouldn't even hear her ringing from inside the house.

What now?

She scanned the perimeter, her eyes locking on the six-foot electric fence surrounding the property. Was it still live? She tossed a bit of grass against it and saw a spark.

Yep. It was live, alright.

She was glad Damian had it activated, but the fact that he was home alone with no real protection made her uneasy.

What if Markov held a grudge? What if he wasn't as far away as they thought?

The immediate threat appeared to be over—Markov had reportedly fled to Central America. But still... her mind raced, imagining all the worst-case scenarios.

She scrutinized the gate and the fence. The gate was lower than the surrounding fence, making it the most feasible entry point. And it wasn't electrified. A glaring weakness in the security setup now that no one was manning it. If Thorn could figure that out, then so could someone with far more malicious intent.

Parking the car off to the side, she climbed over the gate, careful not to catch herself on the jagged spikes at the top. She dropped down silently on the other side and headed up the driveway. The cameras were trained on the gate, but since the feed was directed to the shack, Damian would have no clue she was there. *They really need to fix that security loophole.*

She tried his phone again, but it remained unanswered. Damian was never far from his phone.

Was he okay? Had something happened?

Thorn increased her pace. When she got to the house, she saw that the lounge windows were closed, and the blinds were drawn, blocking any view inside.

Well, she'd just have to knock on the front door like a normal person.

Taking a deep breath, she rapped her knuckles against the wood, the sound unnaturally loud in the still night air. A long moment passed, and she thought maybe he wasn't going to answer.

Panic fluttered in her chest as she imagined him lying there, shot through an open window. Maybe someone had gotten to him. Maybe—

She heard footsteps and let out a shaky breath.

Thank God.

The latch clicked open, and Thorn's heart jumped into her throat.

Would it be too much to throw her arms around his neck and cover him with kisses?

She forced a smile onto her face, though it felt brittle, like it might shatter at any moment. This was it—the moment of truth.

The door creaked open, and there he was. Tall, rugged, darkly handsome—her breath caught. Damn, he was just as gorgeous as she remembered.

"Hi." Her voice came out shakier than she intended, her smile strained. Her heart pounded in her chest, each beat echoing in her ears like a drum. She hadn't been this nervous since she'd gone undercover in Afghanistan two years ago. Back then, the fear of discovery had made her anxious. Now, it was the fear that he'd tell her it was over, that he had moved on.

She bit her lip, fighting to keep her composure.

"Thorn? What are you doing here?" His voice was flat, devoid of the warmth she'd come to expect from him. It hit her like a punch to the gut.

"I—I came to see you. Can we talk?" She searched his

eyes, looking for some sign that he still cared, that he wasn't as closed off as he appeared.

He hesitated, and for a moment, she thought he might let her in. But then his expression hardened, and he shook his head. "I don't think there's anything to talk about."

"What?" Hearing the words was like a knife twisting in her chest. "I don't understand. I thought—"

"Thorn, this isn't really a good time." His expression tightened, the tendons in his neck standing out.

"Why not?" She frowned, confused.

What the hell was going on? Had it all been a lie? Before, in Mexico, had it all been a ploy to get her into bed?

No. She couldn't believe that.

That wasn't the Damian she knew.

Was it?

He took a deep breath, his shoulders tense. "I'm sorry, it's over. I can't be with you anymore."

She stared at him, stunned, confused, totally horrified. Questions unleashed in her mind with the ferocity of a tornado. Sure, they hadn't really spoken since the hotel in Miami, and even then it was just as his protection officer, but still... it wasn't reason to end it. Surely, she deserved more than this?

"Why not?" her voice was a strangled whisper.

"I was feeling trapped. I didn't realize it until I got home, but now that I'm back..." He shrugged. "I don't want to be in that relationship anymore."

Her heart crumpled, blood rushed to her head.

There it was, loud and clear—he was done with her, with all her hot-and-cold bullshit, her mixed emotions, her indecision. She'd made him feel trapped. That stung more than anything.

Yet something inside her wouldn't let it go.

"Damian, please let's talk about this?" Her voice wavered,

and she hated herself for it, hated how vulnerable she sounded but she needed an explanation. He couldn't just switch it off like that, could he? "You owe me that much."

His voice was strained, like he was holding something back. "I owe you nothing. I'm sorry, Thorn. I think you'd better leave."

Leave? Was he frigging serious?

He was kicking her out before they'd even talked. How had she gotten him so wrong?

Thorn blinked, shocked by how cold he was being. She'd thought he'd at least listen to her before cutting her out of his life for good. An icy cold descended as her heart was ripped from her body and crushed mercilessly underfoot. She began to shake as the shock hit.

Fuck him. Fuck everything.

She didn't need this shit in her life.

Except she did.

She needed him so much it hurt. It fucking twisted and burned and tore her apart. An AK unleashing on her soul would do less damage than his words had. Stifling a sob, she turned to leave.

"Go back to Jaden," he called after her. "That's who you belong with. Not me."

She froze, dread pooling in her stomach as his words sank in. Slowly, she turned back to face him, her heart pounding in her chest.

What?

A surge of joy so strong it whipped her breath away shot through her.

Thank you, God.

He wasn't dumping her emotional ass, he was telling her something, sending her message, except she'd been too wrapped up in her own nervousness to see it.

He wasn't alone.

CHAPTER 32

Thorn's mind raced.

Shit. Shit. Shit.

Why hadn't she brought her firearm?

She caught the subtle movement of Damian's eyes, a flicker toward the door. Someone was hiding behind it.

Thorn's instincts kicked in. If Damian was talking like this, there had to be a gun pointed at him. Now she needed to figure out how many threats they were dealing with.

"Are you sure you won't give me one more chance?" she pleaded, emphasizing the word *one*.

He sighed, sounding weary. "I already gave you one chance. There won't be another."

Thorn caught the faint thumbs-up he gave her.

One guy.

She liked those odds.

"Fine, if that's how you want it."

There was no time for backup—she had to act now. In one swift motion, she lunged forward and kicked the door wide open. The man hiding behind it let out a howl as it slammed into his face.

Thorn didn't hesitate. She drove the door into him again, harder this time, feeling it connect with his nose. Blood sprayed across the floor.

"Argh!" he screamed, clutching his face, the pain evident in his voice.

Damian was on him in a flash, grabbing the guy by the collar. Thorn moved with precision, wrestling the gun from his hand. She twisted his wrist sharply, the weapon clattering to the floor as she wrenched it away. With Damian's arm locked around his throat in a tight headlock, the man had no chance to resist.

"Get on your knees!" Thorn commanded, her voice hard and unwavering.

The man collapsed to the ground, still gasping from the impact. As she stared down at him, recognition dawned.

"James?"

It was Damian's head developer, his right-hand man.

James glanced up, blood and snot dripping from his busted nose. "Well done," he sneered, his voice laced with sarcasm.

She didn't appreciate his tone. "Got any duct tape?" she asked Damian, her gaze never leaving James.

"In the kitchen drawer," Damian replied, keeping a firm grip on James.

Thorn moved quickly, retrieving the tape. When she returned, James was squirming, whining about his broken nose.

"Stay still, you little weasel," Damian growled, tightening his hold as Thorn wrapped the tape around James's wrists, securing them tightly.

When she was done, she looked up at James with disdain. "So, you were the leak."

James shot her a venomous look. "Obviously. You think you're so smart, all of you. Meanwhile, I tapped your phone. I installed listening devices in your house. I knew everything you were up to." He laughed bitterly, a grating sound.

"But why?" Damian asked, his voice carrying a note of betrayal. "I thought we were a team?"

"No, Damian. There is no team. There's only you. I deserved more. I helped you build Lydian into a billion-dollar success story, and now you're running it into the ground. All my hard work. I couldn't let you do that."

"So you sold me out to Alek?" Damian's voice hardened, his grip on James's collar tightening.

"How else was I going to get what I deserved? The share price has tanked, millions wiped off the board at the drop of a hat, and all because you had to go all moralistic. What the hell, Damian? What happened to that pioneering spirit? You sold us out, man."

Damian stared at him, disbelief mingling with anger. "Why didn't you come to me? We could have discussed it."

James sneered, his eyes narrowing. "Oh, and you'd have changed your ways for me? I don't think so."

"I could have compensated you. If I'd known you were unhappy—"

"Why settle for compensation when I could have it all?" James's sneer deepened, his eyes gleaming with greed. "The money, the power, the fast cars, the girls…"

Damian frowned, caught off guard. "What girls?"

Thorn's eyebrows shot up in surprise.

"Christine was crazy about you," James spat, glaring at Thorn. "And you ditched her to marry *her*." He nodded at Thorn, clearly clueless that their marriage was just a cover. The listening devices hadn't told him that.

Damian's response was instant and heartfelt. "What can I say? I fell for her."

Thorn swung around. "What?"

His eyes were warm as he smiled at her. "You heard me.

Somewhere along the line I realized you were the one I wanted to be with—permanently."

Thorn's heart soared. The honesty in his words made her want to throw herself into his arms, but she couldn't. Not with James bleeding all over the floor.

Instead, she said, "I love you, Damian Clayton. I just want you to know that—for the record." She wasn't leaving anything unsaid again. "When you said those things... I thought you were breaking up with me. I couldn't handle it."

"I'm sorry. It was necessary. I hoped you'd put two and two together."

Her eyes flashed. "Don't ever give me a fright like that again."

"I won't, I promise."

Thorn grinned, unable to contain her joy. Suddenly, she knew everything was going to be all right.

James groaned loudly. "Hey, I'm still here, you know. Can't you two have this heart-to-heart later?"

"No, we fucking can't," Damian growled, tightening his grip on James. He glanced back at Thorn, a smile tugging at the corners of his mouth. "I'm glad to hear that, because I know this great guy who'd be perfect for you."

She played along, her eyes twinkling. "You do?"

"Yeah, and the best part is, you're already married to him."

She burst out laughing. "I am, aren't I? I keep forgetting that part."

"I so want to kiss you right now," he said, his voice low and rough, "but I can't let go of this jerk."

The jerk in question rolled his eyes, clearly not appreciating being the third wheel.

"Hold that thought," Thorn whispered, as she pulled out her phone to dial 911.

CHAPTER 33

The door had barely shut when Thorn sped across the room and into his arms.

"I missed you so much," she murmured, nuzzling against the warmth of his neck. Her pulse was racing, in tune with her heart.

"Same," Damian replied in a throaty growl that sent shivers down her spine. "It's been a long fucking three weeks."

The hunger in his voice matched her own, the time apart having only stoked the fire that burned between them.

His hands dropped to her hips, gripping her firmly as he lifted her off the ground. She wrapped her legs around his waist, clinging to him like a lifeline as he carried her down the hall to the bedroom.

There was an urgency in their movements, a desperate need to reconnect, to erase the distance that had stretched between them and the fear of the last few hours.

As they reached the bed, however, something shifted. The raw intensity that had driven them so often before gave way to something softer, more tender.

She felt it as he undressed her, removing her shirt slowly, his fingers lingering over the fabric. There was no rush, no desperate frenzy. They had time now.

He undid her buttons one by one, savoring the moment. Next, he peeled off her jeans. When he was done, she was wet and writhing with longing. Only he could make her melt by just looking at her.

She reached for him, needing to feel his skin against hers, to remind herself that this was really happening, that Damian was here, with her.

His shirt came off, and her hands roamed over his chest, feeling the solid muscle beneath her palms. She explored the familiar yet somehow new terrain of his body.

She heard him suck in a breath as she traced the lines of his torso her touch light, reverent.

"Fuck, Thorn," he hissed, his gaze deepening with desire. "I love you too."

She grinned. "I hope so. I was beginning to wonder. I mean, I know we're married and all, but—"

With a growl, he flipped her over and pinned her down on the bed beneath him. She squealed, but he held her firm, and whispered in her ear. "Do you want me to show you how much?"

She nodded, her body weak with longing. She needn't have worried, their attraction hadn't died, it was still there, burning brighter than before.

"I can't hear you." He was taunting her, and she fucking loved it.

"Yes," she pleaded, as he slid her panties off. There was the sound of a zipper coming down and she squirmed, knowing what was coming.

"Yes, what?"

"Yes, please." Her breath was coming in short gasps. She was so completely aroused she couldn't lie still. Tiny shudders of delicious anticipation left her quaking. This was her man, and he was about to claim her in the most primitive way possible.

When he mounted her, her whole world turned upside down. She heard him inhale roughly, and then he was inside her. She was so soaked, he slid in easily, stretching her to accommodate his size.

She was in heaven. Floating in glorious ecstasy. He filled her to capacity, and she didn't know it was possible to feel such a rush of emotions all at once.

Need. Desire. Love.

It all tumbled from her lips in one soft moan. She thought her heart had just burst with happiness.

His rhythm was smooth, hypnotic, and before long she was flying higher and higher, crying out his name with each delicious thrust. She heard him groan as his hips slammed against her ass, driving as deep into her as he could.

With each stroke he sent her stratospheric, until she couldn't bear it anymore.

"Oh, God," she sobbed, as with one last surge she felt him unleash inside her. The heat sent her careening into space, and she heard herself screaming out with pleasure.

Afterwards, he collapsed on top of her, and she could feel his heart thumping through her back. His hands snaked underneath her and he held her tightly, warm in his embrace, until their pulses had returned to normal.

They lay there together, wrapped in each other's arms, letting the quiet of the night settle around them. For the first time in a long time, everything felt right. Everything felt complete.

And as Thorn drifted off to sleep, her head resting against Damian's chest, she knew that whatever challenges lay ahead, they'd face them together—stronger, closer, and more in love than ever before.

CHAPTER 34

*S*ix months later...

THEY GOT MARRIED under the ancient oak tree.

It was a small wedding, just as they had wanted. Pat walked her down the aisle, his arm solid and reassuring beside hers. The rest of the Blackthorn team was there too—Hawk, Anna, and a couple of the guys from the unit who had become more than just colleagues; they were family.

Damian's side was smaller, just a few close friends from the boat club and one or two buddies from his academy, people who meant something to him. Damian was rebuilding his company and had committed to spending more time on his charitable foundation, giving back and helping talented kids make something of their lives.

Thorn wore a different dress this time, one made especially for *him*. It was a delicate, flowing gown of ivory silk that clung to her figure. The bodice was simple yet elegant, with a sweetheart neckline that framed her collarbones, the thin straps resting gently on her shoulders. The back dipped low—just the way he liked it—decorated with intricate lace detailing that added a touch of romanticism.

The look in his eyes as she walked up the aisle on Pat's arm was everything.

"You look stunning," he breathed, reaching for her hand. "But then I've always loved you in a wedding dress."

She laughed, her heart fluttering at his words.

They said their vows under the cobalt blue Californian sky, the air tinged with the scent of the sea and the rustle of the oak's ancient branches above them. There was no one else—just the two of them, promising forever.

"I do," she said, entwining her fingers with his.

God knows I do.

When it was his turn, his gaze never left her face.

Damian slipped the ring on her finger, the birds sang a melody, and they kissed beside the koi pond.

It was perfect.

Afterward, Anna hugged Thorn tightly, whispering something about how happy she was that they'd found each other. Doug, the best man, clapped Damian on the back, grinning widely. "I'm happy for you, man. I mean it." Thorn had gotten to know him over the last few months and liked him a lot. He was the kind of guy who told it like it was and had a heart of gold.

Pat had given her the best wedding present ever. "I'm opening a West Coast branch of Blackthorn Security," he'd told her. "So you can relocate to California."

"Really?" She'd hugged him then, much to his acute embarrassment. Pat didn't do emotion.

"It makes good business sense," he'd said, gruffly.

The FBI still hadn't apprehended Alek Markov, who was rumored to be living off the grid in Panama or somewhere, but they had rounded up a whole bunch of bad guys, thanks to Damian's help, and so his record had been officially expunged. He was finally free.

That's when they'd decided to get married.

They had a small, intimate reception on the patio. Fairy lights twinkled above them, casting a warm glow over the gathering. They danced in each other's arms like there was nobody else around. The world faded away, leaving only the two of them, locked in a moment they would cherish forever.

Finally, one by one, the guests left, drifting away into the night until they were alone.

Damian smiled, and she recognized that gleam in his eye. "How does it feel to be Mrs. Damian Clayton, for real this time?"

She laughed. "It's how I always dreamed it should be."

"No regrets?"

She glanced up at the stars beginning to twinkle in the darkening sky and thought about Jaden. Nothing would diminish what they'd had, but she sensed his presence now, shining down on her. He'd be happy for her, of that she was certain.

"No regrets," she whispered.

WHAT'S NEXT?

Want more Blackthorn Security? Take a look at the next book in the addictive romantic suspense series.

REBEL PROTECTOR

GEMMA FORD

REBEL PROTECTOR

Becca's life is a train wreck. Why is she always drawn to the wrong kind of men? How did she end up working for the biggest crook in Central America? Enter Dom, the charismatic bad-boy mercenary who sets her pulse racing. But when he starts working for her boss, she knows things are about to go from bad to worse...

Undercover agent Dom is on a mission to infiltrate American fugitive Aleksandar Markov's criminal empire. To get close to Markov, Dom seduces the arms dealer's stunning personal assistant, Becca.

When an arms deal goes south and his cover is blown, Dom must risk everything to save the woman he loves—if it isn't already too late.

A sizzling tale of love and suspense in one of the world's most dangerous hot spots.

Available from Amazon and in Kindle Unlimited.

CHAPTER 1

The wheels of the SUV left the tarmac and hit gravel. Dom could hear it kicking up off the surface of the road, bouncing along and hitting the undercarriage. They must be nearly there. It had been a stifling hour-long drive from Panama City with his hands bound behind his back and a sack over his head, but he understood the need for secrecy.

Aleksandar Markov, the new kid on the block and one of the most ruthless arms dealers the region had ever seen, valued his privacy. His hacienda was situated on the Panamanian coast, in the middle of nowhere.

It had taken weeks of negotiation to reach this point. First, Dom had used his contacts in the drug trafficking industry to get in touch with Markov's right-hand man, Luis Ramirez. Then, after being vetted and having his position in the trafficking network verified, he was granted a meeting with Markov.

They had picked him up outside his hotel in Panama City, a squalid hostel that barely deserved its single star, and brought him here—but not before he was patted down and checked for wires and weapons. Now, feeling disoriented and a little carsick, he had arrived at his destination: Alex Markov's secret compound. In a few moments, he'd meet the infamous legend himself.

Markov had arrived six months ago with a cache of illegal arms that he needed to offload. Where the weapons had come from, no one knew. Rumor had it they were from conflict zones in Eastern Europe and Central Asia, where he had a string of black-market contacts. But since the FBI was closing in on his operation, he'd packed up and relocated to Panama, where there was a lucrative trade in illegal arms to guerrilla groups, cartels, and paramilitary organizations in South America.

He had pissed off many established arms dealers in the region, but they had been swiftly dealt with in such a manner that no one was likely to challenge his position again. Markov was here to stay.

The SUV came to a halt, and Dom heard the front passenger door open and someone get out. There were footsteps on gravel, and he braced himself for the unexpected. Always be prepared.

But nothing happened.

A moment later, his door opened, and he was hauled out of the vehicle. Once on his feet, the ties binding his wrists were cut, and the bag was ripped from his head.

Shit, it was bright.

He blinked to adjust his vision. As soon as he could see properly, he looked around, taking stock of his surroundings. They were outside a Spanish-style mansion in a stone courtyard with a fountain in the middle. The property was heavily secured. He immediately spotted two armed guards watching from a respectful but highly accurate distance, not counting the four banditos who'd brought him here, all of whom were packing.

The man who had put the bag over his head was called Carlos. He was an ugly man with a scowling face, a hawkish nose, and lips that seemed molded into a permanent sneer. Dom didn't like him and sure as hell didn't trust him. He didn't know the names of the two thugs he'd cozied up with in the back seat, but they walked off, and the SUV drove around the back, presumably to park.

Dom studied the lavish white Mediterranean residence with its typical red-tiled roof. It was an impressive building, and what it lacked in height, it made up for in breadth. He suspected it stretched back a fair distance, probably all the way to the beach. He could smell the sea; it was no more than five hundred meters away. The salty tang was a welcome relief after the hot stench of Panama City.

The front door opened, and through the expansive archway walked a compact, stocky man in an expensive suit. His hands were clenched into fists, but he made this look natural. He practically sizzled with thinly concealed aggression.

"Mr. Ramirez?" Dom inquired.

The man stretched out his hand. "Mr. Domínguez, welcome to Villa del Mar. I'm sorry for the crude method of delivery, but you know how it is..." He petered off with a non-apologetic shrug.

They shook hands. "I understand."

"Follow me. Mr. Markov is expecting you."

Ramirez nodded at Carlos before turning on his heel and heading back into the house. Dom walked with him under the white arch and through a double-volume, steel-reinforced front door. No one was getting in here without an invitation.

The interior was cool and surprisingly tasteful. Marble tiles, white walls, and top-notch air conditioning all contributed to the ambiance. Luscious indoor plants were strategically placed in darker corners, and the walls were adorned with several pieces of fine modern art.

They descended a short flight of stairs to a formal living area, and through the floor-to-ceiling windows, Dom caught a breathtaking view of the terrace and swimming pool. It was surrounded by natural vegetation, giving it a tropical feel. In the distance, he could see a partial view of the pearly sands of the estate's private beach. It was quite a secret hideaway Markov had here.

Reclining on a sofa, a finger of whiskey in a glass on the coffee table in front of him, was Aleksandar Markov himself. He didn't look anything like Dom had imagined. After all the briefings, he had expected a monster. Instead, Markov was of average height, distinguished, and corporate-looking with a smattering of salt-and-pepper hair. He reminded Dom of a retired city banker.

"Mr. Dominguez, how good of you to come." He even sounded like a banker. His accent was interesting—a mixture of an American twang over a distinctly Eastern European inflection.

Dom stepped forward and shook his hand. It was cool and dry, but the handshake was firm and strong. "Thank you for seeing me." It was the eyes, Dom decided, that betrayed his ruthless nature. Pale blue and colder than the polar ice caps, they were totally devoid of emotion.

"Please, sit down. Becca will bring us some tea." He snorted. "A little habit I picked up when I lived in London many years ago."

Dom glanced up and saw a stunning brunette hovering in the doorway. Glossy brown hair, soft curves, and legs that disappeared under a tight skirt that went on forever. She flashed him an efficient smile and nodded to Markov before disappearing to get the beverages.

Damn. Markov sure knew how to pick them.

Was he sleeping with her? Dom wondered. A stunner like that, he couldn't see how he wasn't. Markov struck him as the kind of man who took what he wanted from life and to hell with the consequences.

Dom turned his attention back to the arms dealer. "It's a beautiful place you have here. I'll bet the sunsets are something else."

Markov smiled and acknowledged the truth of that statement with a small bow of his head. "It's not California, but it'll do." Dom didn't respond. He'd been told Markov had been based in San Francisco, near Silicon Valley, where he'd funded some sort of crypto startup. Apparently, it had been a way to launder his money and allowed him to operate undercover on the dark web. Dom didn't know much about those things, but he got the picture. Markov was an HVT and top of the FBI's Most Wanted list.

"Where do you hail from?" asked Markov. Ramirez poured himself a drink from a liquor cabinet, then took a seat at a modern glass-and-chrome table a few feet away. Markov's partner was an observer in this meeting, not an active participant. It was clear who called the shots.

"Florida, originally," Dom replied, sitting down opposite the arms dealer. "Although I move around a lot."

Markov nodded. It was expected in his line of work.

"Tell me about that." Markov's gaze fixed on Dom's face.

"About what?" Dom knew what he meant, but he played along.

"How did you end up here, in Central America?"

It might seem like a harmless question, but it was an integral part of the interview. Markov had checked him out, but this was the part where he had to live up to his reputation— where he had to sell himself to Markov as someone the arms dealer needed.

"After I left the Army, I was assigned to the U.S. Training

Support Unit in Belize as an instructor in close combat and jungle warfare. That was my specialty back in the military."

"Special Ops, wasn't it?"

Dom was impressed. Markov must have contacts in the DoD to get that kind of information. Usually, Special Forces operatives' names were redacted for their own safety, even after they'd left the service. But since it was out there, he saw no reason to hide it. If anything, it would help his cause.

"Yes, sir. I served ten years in the U.S. Marine Corps and four in MARSOC." MARSOC, or Marine Forces Special Operations Command, was the Marine Corps' special operations unit. They specialized in direct action, special reconnaissance, and counter-terrorism. Its members trained and operated closely with the more famous Navy SEALs.

Markov narrowed his eyes. "So, after fourteen years risking your life for your country, you end up an instructor in a rainforest in the ass end of nowhere? Is that right?"

Dom gritted his teeth. That about summed it up. "Yes, sir."

"What did you do to piss them off?"

Dom remained silent, his entire body tense. This was one step farther than he wanted to go, but he saw the value in it. He'd be a fool not to work this angle. Showing how angry he was about what had happened would sell his cover even more. The best part was, he didn't even need to lie about it.

The stunner returned with the tea and put the tray down in front of them. "Shall I pour, Mr. Markov?"

"Please, Becca."

She bent over, and Dom got a whiff of her perfume. It was light and sensual, like meadow flowers on a summer's day. He watched as she poured the tea into two china cups, admiring the way she moved.

It was like sexy poetry in motion.

Her hair fell forward, but she made no move to tuck it back behind her ears. Suddenly, he wanted to touch it, to slide his hand around the back of her neck and draw her towards him.

Fuck, his fantasy was running away with him.

Sure, it had been a while since he'd had a woman, but still... Now? In the middle of an undercover op? He must need his head examined.

She handed him the tea with the barest hint of a smile. Her eyes were a rich brown flecked with gold, and where Markov's were empty, hers were filled with hidden secrets.

Then she did the same for her boss, this time adding milk and one sugar cube before stirring it thoroughly. How had she known Dom took his black?

"She makes an excellent cuppa for a Yank," Markov remarked once she had left the room. Dom noticed she hadn't offered Ramirez any. "That's one of the reasons I stole her."

"Stole her?" Dom thought he'd misheard.

Markov laughed. "Nothing sinister, I assure you. I poached her from the U.S. Embassy in Panama City. I was there for a meeting, and she served us tea. It was perfect—very rare in this part of the world—so I made her an offer she couldn't refuse. Now she works for me, and to be honest, I couldn't do without her. Becca literally runs my life. Anyway, I digress. You were saying?" He turned his dead eyes back to Dom.

Dom didn't want to know exactly what Becca did for Markov, so he forged ahead with his cover story.

"I was in charge of an op that went south," he explained. "We received some bad intel and stormed an enemy compound, only to find it was a hospital for sick, orphaned kids. It was a major fuck-up. There were no casualties, thank God, but we got caught in one hell of a firefight on the way out. It became an international incident, and my team was held responsible." He couldn't keep the bitterness from his voice.

Markov watched him closely. "You took the blame."

"Yeah, I was the unit commander. I had no choice. Someone's head was going to roll, and it happened to be mine. I was offered the post in Belize because they didn't know what to do with me. I was an embarrassment to the squad—or to the politically motivated powers that governed the unit."

"Is that why you went AWOL?"

Now for the fun bit.

Dom scoffed. "The salary was fucking abysmal, and there was no action. Why would I want to stay in that shithole when I could earn ten times that on the private circuit?"

"As a paid mercenary," Markov added.

"Of sorts," Dom leaned forward, preparing for the hard sell. "Sir, I single-handedly set up Alberto Suarez's distribution ring through the notoriously dangerous Darién Gap between Panama and Colombia. I scouted the route, set up the network, bribed the locals, and then tested and secured it until it was perfect."

"Suarez was caught," Markov pointed out. "He was arrested two weeks ago by the DEA."

"Not on my watch," Dom replied. "And not because of anything I did. He sold his product to the wrong guy—that's what got him busted. He walked straight into a trap. My distribution network is still in place." And therein lay the unique selling point and the sole purpose of this meeting. He let his words sink in.

Markov studied him for a full minute before he replied. "Is that why you're here? You want to work for me?"

Dom took a deep breath. "Since Suarez is out of play, I'm out of a job. I hear you're looking to expand your distribution into Colombia, and I have those routes already in place.

If I can speak plainly, sir?" He glanced at Ramirez and then back at Markov.

Markov nodded. "Whatever you need to say, you can say in front of Ramirez."

Dom continued. "It's perfect for small arms distribution. There are no end-user certificates to forge, the disseminated nature of the network makes it much harder to police, the border is in the middle of impenetrable jungle, impossible to patrol in any orderly fashion, and the best part is, I know how to get the merchandise through without detection."

There was a pause as the relevance of what he was offering sank in. Ramirez glanced at Dom and then to Markov, his eyebrows raised. Still, Markov didn't react.

Dom waited. He picked up his teacup and took a sip. He wasn't the biggest fan, but Markov was right. It was excellently brewed.

"Who'd you hear that from?" Markov asked softly.

Dom met his gaze. "From suppliers we used to deal with on the Colombian end. They told me they're interested in acquiring your weapons to support their cause."

Many of the drug cartels and criminal groups operating in Colombia purchased arms from dealers like Markov. Sometimes they paid with cocaine, other times with cold, hard cash. Either way, it was a lucrative business to be in. Markov was intent on muscling in, and Dom was giving him his chance.

The pale blue eyes flickered over his face, but Dom remained passive. He forced his shoulders to relax. "It's all set up," he reiterated. "You don't have to do anything other than sit back and enjoy the profits. There's a market that wants what you're selling, and I have a way to get it to them with minimal risk."

"It's worth considering," cut in Ramirez, speaking for the first time.

"How do I know you aren't full of shit?" Markov asked.

"Because I worked for Suarez for ten months and helped make him a very rich man. Ask anyone involved in his organization—they'll vouch for me."

"There aren't many left who aren't in jail," Markov retorted.

"Like I said, that had nothing to do with me."

"Why weren't you arrested?" Ramirez directed the question to him.

Dom glanced at him. "Because I'm too smart to go along to a sting." Markov snorted. "My business was the supply end," Dom continued. "I wasn't involved in selling the merchandise. My job was to bring in the product from Colombia, that's it. When I got wind of what had happened, I disappeared. There's nothing linking me to Suarez's organization."

"Smart." Markov drummed his fingers on the side of his empty teacup, his brow furrowed. The seconds ticked by. Eventually, he said, "Okay, I'm interested. Let's set up a trial run and see how it goes."

Dom nodded.

He was in.

Becca, Markov's assistant, returned. "Is there anything else I can get you, sir?" Even her voice was sweet, like honey.

"We're good." He waved her away, and she left the room, but not before shooting a curious, appreciative glance in Dom's direction.

* * *

Enjoyed the extract? *Rebel Protector* is now available from Amazon and Kindle Unlimited here: amazon.com/dp/B0DCC7ZZWF

ABOUT THE AUTHOR

Gemma Ford is a romantic suspense novelist who enjoys writing about feisty, independent women and their brave, warm-hearted men. *Duty Bound* is the first book in Gemma's Blackthorn Security romantic suspense series.

You can browse the rest of the series or sign up to Gemma's mailing list for discounts, promos and the occasional freebie at her website: [www.authorgemmaford.com.](www.authorgemmaford.com)

www.ingramcontent.com/pod-product-compliance
Lightning Source LLC
LaVergne TN
LVHW021701060526
838200LV00050B/2447